THE PEAK
NATIONAL PARK

Roland Smith

Webb & Bower
MICHAEL JOSEPH

Acknowledgements

I would like to record my thanks to John Anfield, Ken
Smith, George Challenger and Andrew Greenwood of the
Peak National Park for kindly checking my manuscript and
offering constructive suggestions, and to Elaine Fisher for
her word processing skills.

Photographs by Mike Williams

First published in Great Britain 1987 by
Webb & Bower (Publishers) Limited
9 Colleton Crescent, Exeter, Devon EX2 4BY
in association with Michael Joseph Limited
27 Wright's Lane, London W8 5SL
and The Countryside Commission,
John Dower House, Crescent Place,
Cheltenham, Glos GL50 3RA

Designed by Ron Pickless

Production by Nick Facer/Rob Kendrew

Illustrations by Rosamund Gendle/Ralph Stobart

Text and new photographs Copyright © The Countryside Commission
Illustrations Copyright © Webb & Bower (Publishers) Ltd.

British Library Cataloguing in Publication Data
The National parks of Britain.
The Peak
1. National parks and reserves — England —
Guide-books 2. England — Description and
travel — 1971-   — Guide-books.
I. Smith, Roland
914.2′04858 SB484.G7.

ISBN 0–86350–135–4

Typeset in Great Britain by Keyspools Ltd., Golborne, Lancs.

Printed and bound in Hong Kong by Mandarin Offset.

Contents

Preface

The Peak is one of ten national parks which were established in the 1950s. These largely upland and coastal areas represent the finest landscapes in England and Wales and present us all with opportunities to savour breathtaking scenery, to take part in invigorating outdoor activities, to experience rural community life, and most importantly, to relax in peaceful surroundings.

The designation of the national parks is the product of those who had the vision, more than fifty years ago, to see that ways were found to ensure that the best of our countryside should be recognized and protected, that the way of life therein should be sustained, and that public access for open air recreation should be encouraged.

As the government planned Britain's post-war reconstruction, John Dower, architect, rambler and national park enthusiast, was asked to report on how the national park ideal adopted in other countries could work for England and Wales. An important consideration was the ownership of land within the parks. Unlike other countries where large tracts of land are in public ownership, and thus national parks can be owned by the nation, here in Britain most of the land within the national parks was, and still is, privately owned. John Dower's report was published in 1945 and its recommendations accepted. Two years later another report drafted by a committee chaired by Sir Arthur Hobhouse proposed an administrative system for the parks, and this was embodied in the National Parks and Access to the Countryside Act 1949.

This Act set up the National Parks Commission to designate national parks and advise on their administration. In 1968 the National Parks Commission became the Countryside Commission but we continue to have national responsibility for our national parks which are administered by local government, either through committees of the county councils or independent planning boards.

This guide to the landscape, settlements and natural history of the Peak National Park is one of a series on all ten parks. As well as helping the visitor appreciate the park and its attractions, the guides outline the achievements and pressures facing the national park authorities today.

Our national parks are a vital asset, and we all have a duty to care for and conserve them. Learning about the parks and their value to us all is a crucial step in creating more awareness of the importance of the national parks so that each of us can play our part in seeing that they are protected for all to enjoy.

Sir Derek Barber, Chairman Countryside Commission

Introduction

The Peak District was the first British national park to be designated, on April 17th, 1951 – and in many respects it was a national park where it was most needed.

Almost completely encircled by Blake's 'dark, Satanic mills' in the great manufacturing cities of the north and Midlands, the Peak stood out as a large green and unspoilt oasis in a spreading desert of industrialization. It was an oasis which was constantly under threat from the ambitions of developers and industrialists.

John Dower, the planner and architect of Britain's national parks system, noted in his seminal report published in 1945, that 'the ever-spreading inferno of limestone quarries and lime-works' was the worst disfigurement of the proposed Peak District National Park.

And two years later, Sir Arthur Hobhouse's Report of the National Parks Committee proposed the Peak as one of the first four British national parks. His report stated: . . . 'beyond its intrinsic qualities, the Peak has a unique value as a National Park, surrounded as it is on all sides by industrial towns and cities. Sheffield, Manchester, Huddersfield, Derby and the Potteries lie on its borders; indeed it is estimated that half the population of England lives within sixty miles of Buxton.'

'There is no other area which has evoked more strenuous public effort to safeguard its beauty. Its very proximity to the industrial towns renders it as vulnerable as it is valuable.'

Reporting to a sympathetic Government which had pledged post-war action on national parks, Hobhouse also regarded mineral extraction as the most serious menace to the Peak's landscape.

He recognized that the area had been worked for lime and for lead since ancient times, but these old workings were on a small scale and had seldom led to major scenic damage: 'But today the increased power of modern machinery is visibly reducing the

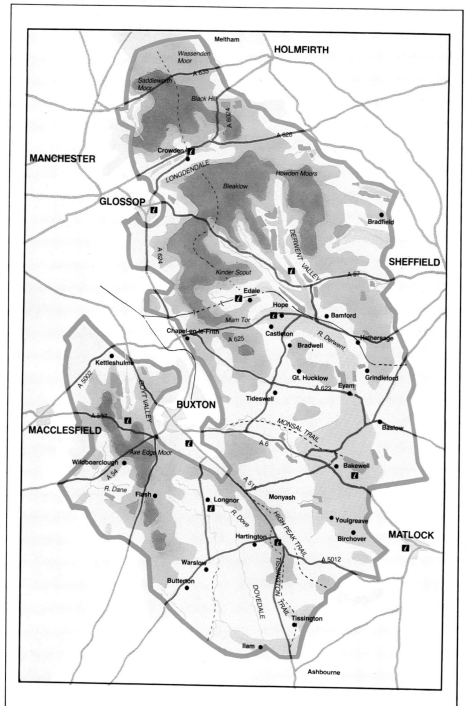

Facing The Peak National Park.

hills and scooping out the fertile soil of the dales at a progressively accelerated rate.'

Having considered evidence from all sides, Hobhouse excluded most of the major workings, with room for expansion, from the area of the proposed park – which accounts for its present odd shape. He thought that there was enough high quality limestone within that area to last for several generations and that it would be possible to exclude any new large-scale quarrying from the park. His conclusion has sadly proved to be over-optimistic.

But the most distressing injury to the Peak landscape because, according to Hobhouse, it could most easily have been avoided, was the unrestricted spread of suburbia from the surrounding cities into places like the Hope Valley. It was perhaps significant that on his retirement after twenty years as chairman of the National Park authority in 1982, the 'Grand Old Man of the Peak' the late Alderman Norman Gratton of Tideswell, could claim the Park's greatest success had been the halting of the spread of the creeping suburbia between Sheffield and Manchester.

The other vital element in the quest to make the Peak one of the first national parks was the tremendous pressure which had built up in the inter-war years for public access to its mountains and moorlands. Generations of mill workers from

Early morning mist in Beresford Dale, one of the least spoilt dales of the White Peak.

The Kinder Scout plateau, seen here from the Woodlands Valley, was the unattainable goal for early ramblers from the surrounding cities. Access was barred by landowners who wanted the moors preserved for grouse.

Manchester and steel men from Sheffield had turned to the open, inviting moors of the Peak as an escape to freedom at the end of their week's toil. Ewan MacColl's famous rallying song, *The Manchester Rambler*, puts it succinctly:

'I may be a wage slave on Monday,
But I am a free man on Sunday.'

These 'ramblers from Manchester way' were in the vanguard of a growing surge among members of what was known as the 'outdoor movement' to reclaim their ancient right to roam freely across such territory. It was a movement, according to Patrick Monkhouse, one of the first members of the Peak National Park Board, with hardly a parallel elsewhere in Britain. 'For an hour on Sunday mornings it looks like Bank Holiday in the Manchester stations, except that families do not go to Blackpool for Whit-week in shorts. South countrymen gasp to look at it.'

And, as he recounts in his *On Foot in the Peak* published in 1932, when they escaped to the moors, they would burst into often tuneless song.

'After six days spent in the workshop, or perched on an office stool, with a choice between whispers and silence, no wonder if they find, in the freedom from walls and roofs, freedom from other restrictions and bonds which lap them round in everyday life.'

But in those days, most of the highest and wildest parts of the Peak – although lying only sixteen miles from the city centres of Manchester or Sheffield – were forbidden country to the walker. Phil Barnes, in his classic propaganda pamphlet of 1934, *Trespassers will be Prosecuted*, pointed out that thirty-seven square miles of Bleaklow and fifteen square miles of Kinder Scout were uncrossed by a public path, and in the whole of the moorland part of the Peak – an area of about 215 square miles – only twelve footpaths exceeded two miles in length.

Prof. C E M Joad, who in *The Untutored Townsman's Invasion of the Country*, published just after the war, claimed that hiking had 'replaced beer as the shortest cut out of Manchester', was forced to add that: 'Upon all this country lies a curse, the curse of the keeper.'

Kinder Scout, at 2,088 ft (636 m) the highest point of the Peak, and Bleaklow, a few feet lower at 2,060 ft (633 m), were both strictly preserved grouse moors, policed by zealous gamekeepers not averse to strong-arm tactics to keep ramblers off. Mass rallies

The dramatic limestone gorge of the Winnats Pass, near Castleton, was the scene of mass rallies of up to 10,000 ramblers and outdoor enthusiasts in the 1920s and 1930s in the campaign for national parks and access to the forbidden moors of the Peak.

were held in the Winnats Pass and Cave Dale in protest at the situation, and in support of national park legislation. The whole issue came inevitably to a head on April 24th, 1932, when a much-publicized mass trespass took place from Hayfield via William Clough to Kinder. As a result of clashes with gamekeepers, five ramblers were later committed to a total of seventeen months of imprisonment by Derby Assizes.

There are conflicting views about the need for, and effectiveness of, this action, which was followed by further sporadic mass trespasses. But the trespassers certainly brought the problem to public notice and served as an important catalyst for the national park movement. Hobhouse reported in 1947: 'The controversy over access to uncultivated lands reaches its height in the Peak, where landowners may draw their most remunerative rents from the lease of grouse moors, and where at the same time large areas are sterilized for water catchment. Many of the finest moorlands, where thousands wish to wander, are closed against 'trespassers' and an altercation with a gamekeeper may often mar a day's serenity. A national park in the Peak District will not justify its name unless this problem is satisfactorily solved.'

Within a few years of its foundation, the Peak National Park authority had negotiated access agreements with landowners, along the lines of those proposed by Dower and Hobhouse, to seventy-six square miles of the northern and eastern moors, including the former 'battlegrounds' of Kinder and Bleaklow.

The Peak District National Park, as designated, covers an area of 542 square miles (1,404 sq km), roughly forty miles from Ashbourne in the south to Meltham in the north and about twenty miles across at its broadest point, between Macclesfield in the west and Chesterfield in the east. About 40,000 people live in it, and the major settlement is Bakewell where the National Park has its headquarters.

It lies at the southernmost extremity of the Pennines, the last knobbly vertebra in what school geography textbooks used to call 'the backbone of England'. It is the most southern of the five northern national parks, linked to the Yorkshire Dales and the Northumberland National Parks by Tom Stephenson's 250 mile (402 km) long-distance footpath, the Pennine Way. The North Pennines Area of Outstanding Natural Beauty, a

The first ramparts of upland Britain, Hen Cloud, an outlier of the Roaches, on the Staffordshire Moors.

potential 'conservation area' in the Hobhouse report, would effectively link these two to the north, leaving the thirty mile gap of what John Dower called 'the Industrial Pennines' between the Peak and the Dales.

What then is the character of this most needed and most visited national park? Current estimates show the Peak receives twenty million visits a year, most still from its traditional users in the surrounding cities.

By the accident of geography, the Peak stands at the crossroads of Britain, one stony face turned towards the softer, cultivated landscapes of the south and east, and another set towards the sterner, more elemental landscapes of the north and west. Indeed, there are few places in Britain where the boundary between the uplands and the lowlands is as pronounced and obvious as it is in the Peak District.

You can see it graphically illustrated as you stand on the serrated gritstone ramparts of the Staffordshire Roaches and look down across the flat, patchwork-quilt landscape of the Cheshire Plain to the glinting Mersey in the west. Or perhaps when travelling through the inky blackness of a winter's night along one of the enclosure roads which cross the vast and mostly trackless East Moors, when the neon lights of Sheffield or Chesterfield suddenly come into view, shining like a field of stars beneath.

Traditionally the Peak has been thought of as two quite distinct, contrasting yet compatible, landscapes which both reflect the rocks beneath. The limestone area is called the 'White Peak' from the predominate colour of the rock, and forms the southern and central core of the Peak District. It is enclosed to the north, east and west by a down-turned horseshoe of Millstone Grit and shales known, in contrast, as the 'Dark Peak'. The Dark Peak moors and valleys cover about three quarters of the total area, and the White Peak, the remaining quarter.

Of the two, the White Peak, a gently rolling plateau cleft by numerous precipitous and spectacular dales, is the face of the Peak more like the lowlands, despite the fact that it averages about 1,000 feet in altitude. Here are still to be found the kind of herb-rich wild flower hay meadows which have all but disappeared from lowland Britain. Plants like the man orchid and stemless thistle are at their north-western limit in Britain in the White Peak, exemplifying the highland/lowland frontier.

The visitor coming from the Midlands and entering the Peak from the bustling little market town of Ashbourne can have little doubt he or she has crossed such a frontier. As an early eighteenth century traveller observed, 'at the summit of the hill it was a top coat colder.'

Gone are the hawthorn-hedged arable fields of the fat, flat Midland shires. In their place, grey drystone walls march slowly up the swelling contours of the land. The landscape immediately takes on a more open appearance, perspectives expand and the views grow grander. Sparse clumps of trees become an almost unexpected bonus in the sweeping grandeur of this breathtaking landscape.

Villages are grouped round their local pond or 'mere', or lie in a relatively sheltered fold in the land, seeming to grow naturally from the native stone of which they are built. Water is a precious commodity on the fast-draining limestone plateau and villagers give thanks for it through the unique summer custom of well-dressing.

The remarkable network of drystone walls which enmeshes the land is probably the most abiding impression visitors from the south have of the White Peak. The pearl-grey stone has been used for constructional purposes in this part of the world for

Dovedale from Thorpe Cloud.

The Manifold Valley from Thor's Cave, with the winding curve of the former Manifold Light Railway in the centre. This has now been converted to a tarmaced walking and riding route.

at least 4,000 years, as the enigmatic Neolithic stone circle of Arbor Low demonstrates. Encouraged by kinder climates than those of today, early man made this his home, and everywhere you look, there is evidence of his passing. Every hill, it seems, is topped by a 'low', the local name for a burial mound, from the Old English 'hlaw', the equivalent of the Yorkshire 'howe' or the Scottish 'law'. Later, the limestone plateau and dales were the centre of a thriving and important lead mining industry, which, with farming, gave Peaklanders a true dual economy.

But the real drama of the White Peak is to be found in the dales, like those of the Manifold, Lathkill, Bradford and, most famous of all, Dovedale.

As John Ruskin observed: 'The whole gift of the country is in its glens. The wide acreage of field or moor above is wholly without interest: it is only in the clefts of it, and the dingles, that the traveller finds his joy.'

Castellated white walls of naked rock rise above native ashwoods, while in the dale floor the rivers exhibit that tantalizing habit of limestone streams, sometimes disappearing mysteriously from sight, only to reappear some miles downstream. Many water-cut limestone dales, like the Winnats Pass or

The yawning entrance to Peak Cavern, the largest cave entrance in Britain, towers over the cottages of Castleton.

Cave Dale near Castleton, are completely dry today.

Where the White Peak meets the Dark, especially around Castleton, yet another unseen and unsuspected landscape exists. This is the Peak's underground, a world of beautiful and impressive caves and caverns. Several of them are open to the public as show caves, while others are strictly the playground of those most esoteric of sportsmen, the cavers.

In other places, like the valley of the Derwent – the major river of the Peak – and the Wye, the transition between White and Dark is much more subtle. Here the rivers run through broad shale valleys clothed with luxuriant woods and punctuated by stately mansions like Chatsworth and Haddon. The richness of these shale valleys is, however, merely a prelude to the more dramatic landscape of the gritstone moors, which form a counterpoint to the limestone in the Peakland symphony.

The Dark Peak is indisputably a part of upland Britain, and forms the south-eastern limit for northern species like the cloudberry, bearberry and mountain hare.

Frowning down on the lush river valleys are broken grey walls of Millstone Grit up to sixty feet high – the famous Peak District 'edges'. They run almost continuously for twelve miles down the

Sunset on Derwent Edge, looking towards Win Hill.

eastern side of the national park from Derwent Edge in the north to Beeley Moor, near Matlock, in the south, providing a grand, high-level promenade for the walker, and some of the best climbing in Britain for the rock gymnast. The 'edges' of the west, like the Roaches, are more broken but nonetheless impressive.

Beyond a series of weirdly-shaped, wind-sculptured tors which top some edges, mile after mile of heather, coarse moor and cotton grass extends to the horizon, the home of red grouse, golden plover and curlew. On the highest moors, like Kinder Scout, Bleaklow and Black Hill, even this sparse vegetation gives way to blanket peat bogs or 'mosses' – the nearest places to a true wilderness in England. Sheltering in the lee of the moors, or in the rocky valleys known as 'cloughs', are small hamlets whose major enterprise is the raising of hardy mountain sheep like the Derbyshire Gritstone and Whitefaced Woodland.

Some of the deeper river valleys of the Dark Peak have attracted water engineers seeking to slake the insatiable thirst of the surrounding cities. They dammed the valleys of the Upper Derwent and Goyt among others, drowning several hamlets and farmsteads under the remorselessly rising waters. About fifty reservoirs create the only major water spaces of the Peak, and an unnatural, while not unlovely landscape is made to seem more alien by the extensive, regimented conifer plantations of the Forestry Commission, which often cloak the valley sides.

So this is the Peak District: a country of contrasts at the crossroads of Britain, and a national park by popular demand. But before we investigate the roots of that infinitely varied Peak scenery, perhaps a word should be said in explanation of the name.

Many people come to the Peak looking in vain for that 'sharply-pointed hill' as defined in Dr Johnson's dictionary, and they are disappointed when they cannot find one. The nearest they come to that dictionary definition are the reef limestone hills of Chrome and Parkhouse, which stand guard over the upper reaches of the Dove, or the shapely pyramids of Lose Hill or Shutlingsloe, where the gritstone dominates.

The earliest name for the area, as recorded in the Anglo-Saxon Chronicle of 924, was Peaclond, and the people who lived there were the Pecsaetan, or 'dwellers of the Peak'. But the Old English word 'peac' meant any kind of hill, and the Peak District

undoubtedly *is* hill country. Authorities as distinguished as Camden, Cotton, Drayton, Defoe and Pepys knew the area simply as 'the Peak'.

The problem was further compounded by the cartographers of the Ordnance Survey, who, on their 1864 First Edition one-inch map, unfortunately but perhaps understandably, named the highest point of the district as 'The Peak'. Anything less like the usually-accepted definition of a peak than the great flat tableland of Kinder Scout would be hard to imagine. It has recently led to the equally misleading plural version of 'the Peaks' arising. Neither, of course, is correct because strictly speaking, the Peak is a district, and not a mountain. And that is why the common modern abbreviation of the Peak National Park is perfectly acceptable, for it has history on its side.

One of the few real Peakland peaks, Chrome Hill, near Hollinsclough, in the valley of the Upper Dove.

1 **The roots of scenery**

Imagine a blue, shallow tropical lagoon extending to the furthest horizon, where waves from a deeper sea break constantly over a fringing reef of coral. You are only a few degrees south of the Equator, so the temperature is well up in the eighties, and the sun, almost overhead, beats down relentlessly from a clear blue sky, and reflects off the limpid water.

The water in the lagoon, which is only a few feet deep, is clean and clear, and as you look down through it you can see forests of sea-lilies gently waving their feathery arms in unison with the timeless current. In other places, the lagoon bottom is covered with a fine shifting sediment of mud formed by the shells and bodies of countless myriads of tiny sea creatures which fall and die in a perpetual underwater drizzle. Worms and molluscs constantly crawl over or burrow under this rich undersea soup of living and dying organisms. Other shellfish with coiled or conical external skeletons flit smoothly above the bottom of the lagoon, wafting their waving tentacles to catch their prey, and using their unique and original form of jet propulsion to get along.

Elsewhere, near the edges of this broad lagoon which stretches some twenty-five miles along by ten

Ilam Rock, Dovedale, an eroded tooth of reef limestone thrusting through the ashwoods.

miles broad, further forests of sea-weeds are building up and trapping more of those constantly dying microscopic sea creatures. Together with the larger shells of the molluscs, bivalves (like mussels) and brachiopods, as they too die and drift to the bottom, these seaweed-based skeletons are building up the fringing reef mounds.

Beyond the reefs, a similar process of living, dying and building up is going on, only more slowly, in the deeper ocean. Nothing, it seems, disturbs this scene of tropical tranquillity.

Suddenly, however, there is a deep, underwater rumbling and the calm waters of the lagoon erupt in a mighty upburst of foam and steam. The peaceful scene of a few moments ago is shattered as the floor of the lagoon is subjected to a volcanic eruption of ferocious intensity. Almost all of the frightening eruption is contained beneath the now turbid waters, and the molten rock flows remorselessly from the undersea vent, covering the lagoon bed with a fluid sheet of bubbling, viscous lava. The sky darkens, and from the clouds of escaping gas, hot ash rains down on the surface, blotting out the sun. Perhaps after a few weeks, or months, the restless earth relents and calm returns to our tropical lagoon. Later, the cooled lava is covered again by the teeming marine organisms which re-occupy the clearing waters, and life returns to normal.

But a normal life for where? Just where have we been to witness this incident in the history of the earth? A South Pacific atoll, perhaps, for the conditions described above are almost exactly paralleled with what is happening there today.

No, we were not on Bikini or Tahiti. We were much closer to Bakewell or Tideswell, but the date was some 325 to 360 million years ago. We were watching in that broad, blue tropical lagoon the formation of what we now know as the White Peak, the central limestone core and heartland of the Peak District.

It is difficult, if not impossible, for today's visitor to comprehend a time-scale of that magnitude, even though the period between the epoch which geologists call the Carboniferous, when almost all our Peakland rocks were laid down, and today has occupied only a tenth of the total age of Planet Earth. How could such conditions ever have existed in our cool, temperate climate, on an island which is over fifty degrees north of the Equator today? It is an incredible story, but today's visitor to the Peak can still come across fragments of evidence which

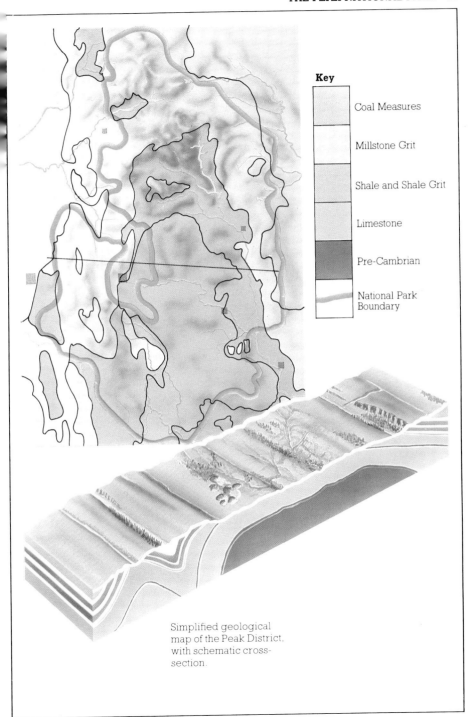

Simplified geological
map of the Peak District,
with schematic cross-
section.

prove that remarkable past.

Just look more closely as you step across one of the numerous 'squeezer' stiles in the drystone walls as you take a White Peak walk. Inspect the individual stones of the wall, or the gate post where cattle have rubbed past. If you are lucky, you will see the stone is completely made up of the fossilized remains of those long-dead sea creatures. The whole wall, walking across the hills, as the Lakeland poet Norman Nicholson has so aptly put it, like a grey millipede on slow stone hooves' is a geological display case, telling us the story of the land.

Crinoidal fossils in a gatepost.

Some fossils look exactly like petrified bolts or beads, with what appears to be a regular screw thread running along their length. Indeed, the local name for these extraordinary fossils is 'Derbyshire screws'.

These are all that remain of those extensive forests of sea lilies in that primeval sea. These strange creatures were not plants at all, but primitive animals, related to modern star fish. They grew on a tall segmented stalk, which could be eight or ten feet in height, and their five branching arms spread out like the fronds of a palm tree to catch both the life-giving, although diffuse, rays of the sun and the tiny sea organisms on which they fed. Those mysterious 'screws' are what is left of their stalks – and tangible proof of the incredibly ancient submarine origins of the rock. During the last century, this 'crinoidal' limestone (the sea lilies are known to geologists as 'crinoids') was much in demand for ornamental purposes, providing stone for fireplaces, floors, washstand tops and window sills and surrounds. When it was cut and highly polished, it showed interesting and varied cross-sections of the stems and was much admired and sold as a kind of 'marble' to Victorians. Examples can be seen in many stately homes, including Chatsworth in the Peak. More recently, it was used to floor the new Cathedral of St Michael in Coventry.

Other fossils often to be seen either in wall stones or in the faces of limestone crags in the dales or quarries include goniatites (rather like the pearly nautilus found today in the warm waters of the Pacific); brachiopods; mussel-like bivalves and thin, pipe-like or fan-shaped corals, like those of the Great Barrier Reef off Australia's eastern seaboard.

In those far-off Carboniferous days, England was part of a huge North Atlantic Continent just south of the Equator, but gradually over the last 300 million

The River Wye in Chee Dale has cut through the bedding planes of limestone to create some of the loveliest river scenery in Britain.

years, it has drifted north on its continental plate to its present position. Nothing in geology is forever, and that tropical paradise was merely one incident – albeit a substantial one of about thirty-five million years – in the story of the Peak. Those millions of tiny sea creatures left layers of limestone (for that is what they formed) over 2,000 ft (608 m) thick in places in the Peak District, and gave us the whiteness of the White Peak.

You can see cross-sections of these bedded limestones in many dale sides, such as along the valley of the River Wye in Millers Dale, Chee Dale and the charmingly-named Water-cum-Jolly Dale; and in Stoney Middleton Dale, where the joints or bedding planes of the various stages of deposition can clearly be seen in terraces in the rock face.

Nowadays, they provide useful belaying points for rock climbers scaling the precipitous walls.

The fossil-rich reef limestones which fringed the lagoon were generally more resistant to the forces of erosion, so they have tended to leave more isolated and distinctive hills, including the nearest approaches to real peaks in the Peak District.

These include a whole series in Dovedale. The river flows a meandering course between a series of limestone reef knolls including the sharply-pointed Chrome and Parkhouse Hills at its upper (northern) end; Raven Tor, Pickering Tor and Tissington Spires in its middle section; finally to emerge between the twin shapely portals of Bunster Hill and Thorpe Cloud in the south. Other reef knolls exist around Castleton, at Treak Cliff, now honeycombed by caves; the Winnats Pass; Cave Dale, and the hill on which Peveril Castle stands with Peak Cavern yawning beneath.

This translucent bowl is a beautiful example of skilfully worked Blue John.

But what of those submarine volcanoes which shook the peace of our tropical, Carboniferous lagoon? Their lavas formed a dark, green-blue rock called basalt, often containing calcite-filled gas bubbles which give away the fiery nature of its birth. These ancient lavas, rarely more than sixty feet deep in the Peak District, are locally known as 'toadstones'. There are several explanations of this strange name, but the one I favour is a typically Peakland term of disparagement which could well have been given it by the old lead miners when they came across the useless material: 't'owd stone'.

You can see examples of basalt outcrops at the aptly-named Black Rock Corner west of Ashford-in-the-Water on the Buxton road; in the reef formations of Cave Dale, Castleton, and in the quarries near the former station buildings in Millers Dale. In Tideswell Dale, a bed of clay overlaid by lava was baked by the heat and split into hexagonal columns just like the basalts of the more famous Fingal's Cave, on Staffa in the Hebrides.

The lead that those miners were looking for is just one of a number of minerals which occur in veins in the limestone. They were formed as hot solutions were forced from the molten inner core of the earth into the many cavities in the rock. As they cooled, the minerals crystallized to create galena (lead ore); fluorspar, such as the rare and beautiful Blue John stone found only around Castleton; barytes; calcite and copper, which was mined extensively at Ecton Hill, in the Manifold Valley. Of these, lead has proved to be the most important in terms of the mineral wealth of the Peak. It has been mined at least since Roman times, and the workings of the old lead miners, which reached their zenith during the 18th and 19th centuries, have left an indelible mark on the White Peak landscape. Everywhere you look on the limestone plateau, and even in some dale sides, you can still see signs of this industry, which doubled with livestock farming in the economy of many Peak District families.

Those immensely thick layers of limestone form the bedrock of the Peak and rest, in turn, on even older massive rocks which go back to the dawn of the Earth. But the white-grey limestone, weathered into the gently swelling White Peak plateau, is the oldest rock now visible in the Peak District. To find out what happened next in the chequered geological history of the Peak, we must go back again to that shallow, limestone-forming sea of the Carboniferous era.

Two hundred miles to the north, the forerunners of what are now the Scottish Highlands were being formed from the immensely old foundation rocks of the North Atlantic continent. The uplifting of these mountains gave rise to large rivers flowing off them southwards into the shallow sea which was covering what is now the Peak and Pennines. In the fresh waters of these Caledonian rivers, vast quantities of debris, in the form of fine sand, grit, silty mud and pebbles were washed down and spilled out into the relatively clear waters of the sea. Over millions of years, these 'Scottish' sediments formed huge, fan-shaped deltas superimposed over the shelly, limestone beds of the lagoon and reefs.

To use another comparison with the present, the Peak would have looked at that time rather like the Gulf of Mexico, with the muddy Mississippi flowing into it, or the Mediterranean near the delta of the Nile. Occasionally, other earth movements would tilt or raise the highlands causing different patterns of distribution of the sediments; sometimes the waters would be clear and sometimes more turbid, and shifting currents would ripple the fluid surface. At times, the Peak would have resembled an extensive fen-land of low-lying mudflats, swamps or sandbanks standing proud of the brackish water. Winds would carry the spores and seeds of primitive, fern-like land plants on to this virgin territory, and they quickly germinated in the warm, moist climate. The subsequent forests of giant tree ferns and huge 'calamites' (sixty-foot ancestors of our modern horse-tails) would become the Coal

Measures on which Britain's industrial empire was built. It is fascinating to think that the closest modern relatives of these giant, scale-covered trees are the insignificant horse-tail, or the rare stag's horn clubmoss, still found in miniscule form on isolated moorland localities around the Hope Valley.

The Coal Measures never reached the thicknesses in the Peak that they did in the surrounding lowlands, although occasional outcropping seams are found, such as those near Derbyshire Bridge in the Goyt Valley, or on Goldsitch Moss in the Roaches syncline. They gave us the name of the period – Carboniferous, which means coal-forming.

The alternating layers of sand, mud and grit, compressed into a huge 'sandwich' by succeeding coverings, became the shales, siltstones and sandstones of today's Dark Peak. The succession

The first snows of winter dust icing sugar on the layered sandwich cake of the east face of Mam Tor, the Shivering Mountain, near Castleton.

happened many times, and is graphically illustrated in the striated east face of Mam Tor, the so-called 'Shivering Mountain' which watches over Castleton. The layers, just like the filling in a giant sandwich cake, are exposed in the huge landslip which has sliced a section through the strata of the Peak as cleanly as if by some celestial cakeknife. They are best seen in the failing light of evening, or after a light dusting of snow, which adds 'icing sugar' to the sandwich. The name 'Shivering Mountain' gives a clue to the unstable nature of these thin layers. They

The Tower, Alport Castles. Not a medieval fortress, this is a huge landslip of unstable shales and grit which overlooks the Alport Valley.

are very loose and friable and constantly break off and fall away. When water seeps between them, catastrophic landslips result, like that which finally swept away the A625 Castleton–Chapel-en-le-Frith road below Mam Tor in 1977. Further extensive slipping can also be seen to the north and west of Mam Tor, in the Edale valley, and further along the ridge at Back Tor, which also shows alternating layers of shale, silt and sandstone in its northern face. A bigger and even more spectacular landslip – said to be one of the largest in Britain – formed Alport Castles, in the side valley of the Alport river, off the Woodlands Valley further north. Here, the isolated, crumbling rocks of the Tower give the appearance of a ruined fortification. Lud's Church, an atmospheric gritstone chasm in the depths of Back Forest, near Gradbach is another example of a landslip, which was a popular Victorian 'sight' and

has been identified as the 'Green Chapel' in the medieval alliterative poem, 'Sir Gawain and the Green Knight'.

The more gritty sands and gravels swept down from the northern mountains, were compressed and solidified to create the Millstone Grit, or gritstone as it is commonly known, of the Peakland 'edges', Kinder Scout, Bleaklow and Black Hill, and provides, along with limestone, the predominate rock types of the Pennines. These coarse sandstones, sometimes containing water-worn pebbles or grains of quartz or feldspar which glint and sparkle in the sun when weathered back down to their original sandy state on paths or in the beds of cloughs, are the foundation of the brooding Dark Peak moorlands.

The impressive 'edges' of Derwent, Stanage, Froggatt, Curbar and Baslow are all formed of Millstone Grit. On the boulder-strewn and bracken-covered slopes beneath their sixty-foot walls can still be found the remains of the industry which gave the rock its name. Piles of discarded, unwanted millstones or grindstones are piled against one another, or can be found half-fashioned in the living rock. The coarse, abrasive nature of the rock made it ideally suited for use in the thousands of corn mills which once existed all over Britain. Later, Peakland

Curbar Edge frowns down on the village of the same name in the Derwent Valley. These cliffs are a favourite spot for rock climbers, while walkers can enjoy a splendid promenade along the top.

Relics of a former industry, these abandoned millstones are below the aptly named Millstone Edge at Lawrencefield, near Padley.

Millstone put to a new use—as a boundary marker of the national park.

grindstones were used to sharpen the products of 'the little mesters' of neighbouring Sheffield's famous cutlery and iron and steel industries. The massive millstones were cut and dressed on site, and a makeshift wooden axle was placed through the central hole as they could be rolled, two by two, down the hillside to the waiting transport. The coming of the synthetic carborundum grindstones killed off the millstone market, hence the abundant abandoned stones.

Visitors see an interesting more modern use for these relics of an ancient industry in the millstone boundary markers of the Peak National Park, since adopted as the logo of the Park authority. It reflects the fact that the Peak has always had a working, industrial base, as well as being an area of exceptional natural beauty.

The 'edges' of the western boundary of the Peak are more complicated, folded and broken than those in the east. But the impressive, wild landscapes of Hen Cloud, the Roaches, and Ramshaw Rocks are all formed of exactly the same kind of sandstones as those in the east.

It is a material which can be cut and dressed quite easily, and is commonly used in local buildings, even in limestone country. Some blocks split readily

along their bedding planes, to form stone slates for roofs, while others have been used for setts and kerbs in roadmaking all over Britain. Gritstone quarries, however, are now rare, and always on a much smaller scale than the massive limestone quarries which are eating away around the edges of the White Peak.

Above the 'edges', in places like Derwent Edge, around the rim of Kinder Scout and Bleaklow, and at Ramshaw Rocks above the Leek–Buxton road, the gritstone is often eroded into exotically sculptured tors. It is an unexplained oddity why this word 'tor', from the Old English meaning a high rock or rocky hill, is not found elsewhere in Britain apart from in the Peak and in the West Country. Limestone cliffs, like Raven's Tor in Dovedale and Chee Tor along the Wye, also adopt the name.

Gritstone tors are the weathered remnants of harder rock which was rotted and weakened along its joints and planes underground, to be exposed and finally modelled by the wind, rain, frost and thaw in later ages. These powerful agencies have produced an extraordinary range of shapes and formations, like the Eagle Stone above Baslow Edge, the Salt Cellar and Cakes of Bread on Derwent Edge, and the Boxing Glove Stones and Woolpacks on Kinder.

Noe Stool, one of the many gritstone tors which ring the plateau of Kinder Scout.

The Millstone Grit uplands, which form the highest and wildest parts of the Peak District, are formed of a rock much more impervious to water than the jointed beds of limestone, so the peat-covered moorlands which mark them are badly-drained, boggy places usually unsuited to cultivation. But these places form the last great wilderness of the Peak, and are the joy of those hardy Sheffield and Manchester ramblers. How many of them realize however, the rock on which they stand to admire the tremendous views across moor and dale at 2,000 ft (608 m) above the sea was once a sandbank on the edge of a prehistoric ocean?

As already explained, the Millstone Grit was the last level of these sedimentary rocks (i.e. laid down under the sea) to be deposited. So why does it not cover the whole of the Peak, why are the deeper and older limestones exposed in the White Peak, and how were the dales and shale valleys formed?

To find the answers to these questions in the Peak District conundrum, two other forces of nature, one constructive and the other destructive, must be understood.

After the various Carboniferous rocks were formed, they came under the combined influences of two opposing forces, one from below and the other from above. The first, that of folding, threw up the limestone-shale-gritstone 'sandwich' of the southern Pennines into a dome, usually known as the Derbyshire Dome. Movements deep within the earth compressed the crust of rocks together – just like crumpling a flat tablecloth – to push up a ridge in the middle. The western side of the Peak, as already explained, was more crumpled into a series of more narrow north–south folds than the east, and was therefore subject to more fracturing and faulting. This great arch of strata could have reached an Alpine height of 10,000 ft (3,040 m) at its highest point in the centre and sloped gradually off to the east and west.

Almost immediately, however, those subtle yet all-powerful forces of erosion set to work breaking down those heights by the combined action of frost, rain and running water. Because they were on top of the sandwich, it was the Coal Measures, shale and Millstone Grit in the centre which were worn away first, exposing the limestones beneath.

Eventually, perhaps 220 million years ago, the surface plan of the Peak that we see today was established. It takes the form of an elongated southern oval of limestone, bounded on the west, east and north by Millstone Grit and shales. It can be compared to the balding pate of a man, with the limestone the exposed scalp in the centre, and the gritstone, the remains of his hair on the back and sides.

During the Permian and Triassic periods (between 280 and 195 million years ago) the Peak, like the rest of Britain, was covered by the drifting sand dunes of a desert much like the present Sahara. Then for perhaps another 100 million years, it was submerged yet again beneath the seas of the Jurassic period. The age of the dinosaurs left little or no mark on the Peak District landscape, and erosive forces have swept away deposits left by the Permian and Triassic periods. Only in isolated pockets on the limestone plateau, such as at Friden, near Newhaven, are deposits of silica sands which probably date from the intervening Tertiary period, of between two and seventy million years ago.

The last great destructive forces which have shaped the Peak District landscape were those of the glaciers during the Ice Ages. The Great Ice Age of the Pleistocene period, which started perhaps a million years ago – only yesterday on the geological time-scale – provided the final finishing touches to Nature's masterpiece. From the rough-hewn matrix of that 300 million-year-old model, it was left to the gouging, crushing, and finally melting powers of the ice to carve the delicate details of the Peak we see today.

In fact, there were several advances of the Arctic ice sheet from the north, with relatively warm interglacial periods lasting perhaps thousands of years in between. Glaciers probably only totally covered the Peak District on two occasions during the Ice Ages, in the glaciations known to geologists as the Anglian and Wolstonian. During the last, Devensian, glaciation, the Peak experienced nothing more severe than a very cold, tundra-type climate, with extensive snowfields but no permanent ice cover.

The southern Pennines were usually at the limit of these vast northern glaciers, so by the time the ice reached the Peak, it was very slow-moving and had lost much of its abrasive, erosive force. In fact, the glaciers were depositing rather than eroding.

The ice brought with it vast quantities of ground-down debris, rocks and stones, which it had picked up in its journey down from the highlands further north. This debris, in the form of a sticky, glutinous

Frost-shattered limestone crags in the upper reaches of Lathkill Dale bear evidence of the powerful forces of natural erosion.

clay known as boulder clay (or till) or rocks and stones carried far from their place of origin and known as 'erratics', can still be found in the Peak, showing the passing of the glaciers. The clay is present around the head of the River Manifold, in Staffordshire, and in the sides of the valley of the River Wye around Bakewell, especially in the notoriously muddy playing fields of Lady Manners School above the town. Here and there, erratic boulders from as far away as the Lake District, the Irish Sea and Scotland have been found, showing the enormous carrying power of those glaciers.

The blanket covering of clay, combined with a layer of wind-blown dust (or 'loess') deposited during the last, Devensian, cold phase gave the limestone plateau a fertile covering of soil. This is one reason why the White Peak has such a green and pastoral appearance, unlike the more spectacular limestone features of the northern Pennines. The dramatic limestone scars and fretted limestone pavements, such a fascinating feature of the Yorkshire Dales National Park, are partly the product of a highly active and erosive ice cover during the last glaciation, while the Peak escaped largely untouched.

It was the Ice Age glaciers, however, which set the pattern of the river systems of the Peak. After each retreat of the ice, or thawing of the snowfields, vast quantities of freezing melt water flowed across the uneven plateau, cutting through the strata of limestone or gritstone like the proverbial knife through butter. This was the time of the genesis of the dales, and the stupendous power of those icy floods is witnessed in the tremendous chasms of the Winnats and Cave Dale near Castleton, cut through reef knolls of limestone.

Many dales, like the two just mentioned, are dry today, while others, like those of the Manifold and Hamps have rivers which at times flow across the surface and then suddenly disappear underground. The Manifold, for example, sinks into its limestone bed near Wetton, only to reappear about four miles downstream in the grounds of Ilam Hall. These eccentricities are a classic feature of some limestone rivers, and the Lathkill is only kept above the surface at its lower end by artificial clay 'puddling' of its bed. The reason for this, however, is partly due to a general lowering of the water table caused by the drainage of lead mines.

It is hard to believe the now-gentle waters of the Dove could have created the dramatic limestone gorge of Wolfscote Dale.

The broad valleys of the Derwent and lower Wye were formed when the softer intervening shales were subjected to the same huge erosive volumes of melt water. A retreating glacier is thought to have changed the course of the Peak's major river, the Derwent, during the Ice Ages. At one time, it is thought the river flowed west of Chatsworth and Calton Pastures and through the present site of Bakewell. The intrusion of a 'Wye Glacier' from the north-west covered Bakewell and interrupted this course, creating a glacial lake near Calver. Eventually, this lake overflowed through what is now Chatsworth Park, and the river adopted its present course, with the Wye eventually rejoining it near Rowsley when the glacier retreated.

Melt water from the retreating glaciers also played an important role in the creation of the many caves in the limestone of the White Peak. The jointed nature of the rock, together with the corrosive effect of acidic rainwater on the calcium carbonate of the limestone and the many cavities already caused by mineral veins, have over millions of years created the Peak's 'underground'. Around Castleton, where some of the finest subterranean scenery is to be found, the caves have become a major tourist attraction. Four caves are open to the public, together with another, the Bagshawe Cavern, at nearby Bradwell. Guided tours around the caves of Treak Cliff, Blue John, Speedwell and Peak Cavern give the visitor a fascinating insight into cave formation, and the stunning beauty of stalactite and stalagmite.

By the end of the Ice Ages, over 10,000 years ago, the Peak was a comparatively barren landscape, with a few stunted trees and low-lying sedges and mosses. Remains found in some caves, such as Windy Knoll below Mam Tor, show that predators like brown bear, wolves, hyaenas and foxes used the caves as dens, and preyed on the exotic Ice Age mammals like mammoth, woolly rhinoceros, reindeer, wild ox and red deer, which grazed the tundra.

We can gain some clues about what the landscape looked like then from the microscopic analysis of pollen samples, taken from the peaty soils particularly in the Dark Peak. One of the earliest experiments of this kind was carried out at Ringinglow Bog, east of Stanage Edge on the eastern moors. Similar experiments have been carried out in the peat bogs of Kinder Scout and Bleaklow and on Totley Moss.

The experiments have shown that arctic willow and dwarf birch were the only trees as the ice retreated, but there was a beautiful, arctic-alpine flora including white-flowering mountain avens. Later, milder conditions allowed hairy birch, aspen and dwarf juniper to establish themselves, while two trees which are still important in the Peak landscape – silver birch and rowan – also first colonized the area. Rockrose and Jacob's ladder, still to be found in the limestone dales, also appeared for the first time during this relatively-warm 'Pre-Boreal' period, of between 8,300 and 7,600 BC.

The climate was steadily improving by this time, and in the Boreal period (between 7,600 and 5,500 BC) an open woodland of Scots pine, birch and hazel existed over most of the moorland plateau, with an extensive fern covering beneath. Other 'modern' trees such as oak, elm, lime and alder appeared to be responding to the kinder conditions and were moving in to the sheltered cloughs and valleys. Pollen surveys done on the limestone plateau (which are more difficult because of the alkaline soil conditions) seem to show less tree cover, with hazel, oak and alder predominating, and ash more prolific in the dales, as today.

The stage was now set for the arrival of perhaps the most important single influence on the landscape of the Peak. This lightly-wooded landscape was waiting for the handiwork of an agent who has affected, in one way or another, every Peak District landscape. That agent was Man.

2 **The dawn of history**

One of my most treasured possessions is a tiny sliver of flint, no bigger than my fingernail. It is the only kind of rock I was used to as a youngster, born and brought up in the arable expanses of East Anglia – but that is not the reason for its importance to me. It assumes its unlikely distinction purely through the circumstances of its finding.

It was on one of those grey 'claggy' days so common in the Dark Peak – a day when the mist constantly threatened, exaggerating the size of the outcropping tors and magnifying the slightest sound, especially the staccato 'go-back' warning of the grouse. It was a day when your imagination could run away with you, especially where we were walking on the peaty wastes of the aptly-named Black Hill in the far north of the national park. John Hillaby, the walker and botanist, accurately described Black Hill as 'a monstrous chocolate cake of peat ringed by the candle-like heads of cotton-grass'. The fellwanderer Alfred Wainwright was more uncharitable. 'It is not the only fell with a summit of peat, but no other shows such a desolate

Peat hags and groughs on Black Hill, looking north east towards Holmfirth.

and hopeless quagmire to the sky.'

It was my first time on Black Hill, and I was glad to be in the company of the local district ranger, who knew these brooding, malevolent moors intimately. We'd already passed the wreckage of a World War Two aircraft, its shining aluminium emerging from the sticky peat of a grough (the local name for a drainage channel in the peat), and we were heading for the thin needle of the Holme Moss television mast, the top of which was deftly threading the shifting mists.

Then suddenly, as can often happen on these unpredictable heights, the mists were swept aside by a kindly westerly breeze, revealing the folded sepia wastes of Wessenden Head Moor and the industrial sprawl of the Tame valley below. It was then, as we crossed one of the many branching streamlets, which in this part of the Peak take the Old Norse name of 'grain', that I came across that tiny, apparently insignificant flint.

It was lying on one of the fluted dunes of chocolate-brown peat, revealed after being buried for perhaps 8,000 years, when the peat bogs started to form. I am sure it was my familiarity with the stone, and the totally unexpected sensation of finding it there, so many miles from the nearest natural outcrop of flint (probably on the Yorkshire

The mast of Holme Moss television station, with its modern replacement, from the 'hopeless quagmire' of Black Hill.

or Lincolnshire Wolds), which attracted my eyes to it.

I picked it up with the sudden realization that I was probably the first person to handle it since a Mesolithic hunter had first fixed it to his arrow and then fired it in pursuit of whatever game had been his quarry in those far-off days of prehistory. It was a humbling experience, perhaps heightened by the wild situation and those shifting, mysterious mists, but I still feel echoes of it even today when I hold that tiny flake of flint.

There are slight traces of Palaeolithic (Old Stone Age) man in caves and rock shelters in the White Peak, notably the flint blades and worked reindeer bones found in the One Ash Rock Shelter in Lathkill Dale, and the caves and shelters of the Manifold and Dove Valleys. As the glaciers of the Ice Ages slowly receded, the first Britons crossed the land bridge from Europe, but they only seem to have ventured into these barren uplands on hunting trips during the warmer summer periods. They may have travelled up the main river valleys in search of horse, reindeer, red deer and bison, and the richest remains have been found to the east of the Peak in the caves of Creswell Crags, now on the Derbyshire/Nottinghamshire border. Here, where the first British evidence of Man as an artist has been found in the shape of a rib bone engraved with a horse's head, remains of animals of the Pleistocene period – mammoth, woolly rhinoceros, wolverine, arctic fox and reindeer – have also been found in the caves of the Magnesian Limestone gorge.

Archaeologists believe these hunters conducted a nomadic type of existence, similar to that of present-day Eskimos, by following migrating herds of the animals which were the major source of their food and clothing. This Old Stone Age 'Creswellian' culture left distinctive artefacts made from local materials, like bone needles and flint tools, which have been recovered in those caves and rock shelters in the sides of the dales. Finds from Thor's Fissure, Elder Bush and Ossom's Caves in the Manifold Valley and Dowel Dale in the Upper Dove, show these early hunters enjoyed a diet of wild horse meat, deer, bison, hare, birds (black grouse and ptarmigan) and fish, so game appears to have been plentiful.

Between 8,300 and 5,500 BC, significant changes were taking place in the climate, and milder, moister conditions led to the open, tundra-like landscape gradually being replaced by forests. This is the period known as the Mesolithic (Middle

Palaeolithic (Old Stone Age) flints from caves in the Manifold Valley.

Stone Age), when bands of hunter-gatherers in small, mobile family communities roamed freely across the open woodlands of pine, birch, willow and hazel on what are now the northern moors. The climate in this Boreal period gradually became relatively warm and dry which made these now-bleak uplands more inviting to the first settlers. The plentiful supply of fruits and nuts from the shrubs and trees of the Millstone Grit plateaux and cloughs must have been another important factor in the colonization of the area, for they formed an important part of the diet of these Mesolithic tribes.

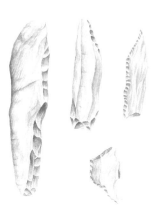

Mesolithic (Middle Stone Age) flint implements from the Wetton Mill rock shelter, Manifold Valley.

But they were also hunters, and that tiny flint microlith which I picked up on Black Hill was not by any means a rare find on the peat mosses of the Dark Peak. Many scatters of such Mesolithic flints have been found on open sites on the high moorlands, usually between 725 and 1,725 ft (220–524 m) above the sea. The frequency of such finds suggest that these areas may have supported a considerable population. Many of the sites of these flint scatters appear to be on exposed hill tops, often commanding extensive views over the surrounding river valleys – just like those across Wessenden Head where I found my microlith.

These microliths look nothing like the classic leaf-shaped arrowheads of later times. They are skilfully-shaped rectangular or trapezoid implements, made from a larger blade of flint. One or more of these flints were fixed on to the wooden arrow shaft, to serve as the barbs. Similar flints were also used as barbs for spears, while other flakes and blades were used as cutting tools and scrapers in the preparation of meat or skins.

So we can imagine these small bands of hunter-gatherers, who probably migrated to Britain from Scandinavia or the Low Countries, scratching a living and roaming across Black Hill, Kinder Scout and Bleaklow. Occasionally, traces of charcoal show where they made fires as they followed the browsing herds of deer and wild horses.

More recent archaeological evidence suggests that these Mesolithic tribes also used fire in another way, not just for warmth and cooking. The suggestion is that they systematically burnt areas of vegetation either to reduce the forest cover and make hunting more easy, or to improve the grazing potential of the land for the animals which were their main prey. Experiments have shown that controlled burning significantly improves the grazing potential of the burnt area, with subsequent increases in its attraction to grazing animals. It was therefore very much to the benefit of the Mesolithic groups to keep certain areas clear of forest, and over the centuries, such practices must have had a considerable impact on the landscape. It is strange to think that similar methods are still used on these same moors today, but the modern system of heather burning is done purely for the benefit of one bird – the red grouse – to stimulate heather growth which should result in increased 'bags' after 'the Glorious Twelfth' of August.

Evidence of the Mesolithic population in limestone areas is sparse, with most finds limited to the same kind of cave and rock shelters used earlier in the Manifold Valley, at Wetton Mill, and at Calling Low in Lathkill Dale. But there may also have been some 'economic' activity in the dales because many of those Mesolithic microliths were not only made of imported flint, but also of black or grey chert, found only in the limestone. Chert axes found in Lathkill Dale and on the plateau at Stoney Low, near Sheldon, may indicate some tree felling, or they could simply have been used for grubbing up edible roots.

For some of the earliest evidence of man as a farmer in the Peak District, we have to return to that narrow, steep fissure known as Dowel Cave in the spectacular valley of the Upper Dove, already mentioned for its Palaeolithic remains. Here, among the layers of silt, clay and gravel were found not only the buried remains of ten people, from a small baby to an elderly man together with the flints and fragments of pottery they might have used, but the bones of domesticated animals.

Those bones included those of sheep or goat, pig and the headless body of a dog. For the first time, it appears that man had settled into a pastoral life-style, and the earliest Peak district farmers and shepherds can be recognized, making their permanent home below the saw-toothed limestone summits of Chrome and Parkhouse Hills – known locally as 'the Dragon's Back'. Even today, especially when the mists rise and wreath these sharply pointed summits, it is not difficult to transport yourself back to those far-off days in this remote and evocative valley. You can imagine those often slightly-built people herding their flocks of sheep and herds of goats and pigs in the newly-cleared meadows won from the surrounding wildwood. The sheep and goats may only have been kept for their milk, and the large areas of

forest would have provided excellent forage – or
'pannage' – for the herds of pigs roaming freely
across the plateau, which would also have speeded
the decline of the woodland. Pollen and snail shell
analysis also indicate an increase in open ground
plants, with cereal crops like wheat and barley with
their associated weeds, making a first appearance.
Farming had truly arrived in the Peak.

We have moved on from the days of the
Mesolithic hunter-gatherers and into the Neolithic,
or New Stone Age to meet these first farmers. There
was no sudden change or invasion by these pastoral
herdsmen, but the concept of farming probably
spread slowly up from the lowlands of the south,
east and west. Indeed, the relatively inhospitable
and isolated nature of the uplands of the Peak may
have been a thousand years later than many other
parts of Britain in witnessing this Neolithic
agricultural 'revolution'. Archaeologists date the
coming of the farmers to the Peak at around
3,000 BC, whereas the usually-accepted date for
lowland Britain is between 3,500 and 5,000 BC. The
cultivation of plants and keeping of animals may
have been forced on these Neolithic tribes to solve
the problems of diminishing hunting resources.

These people not only introduced the skills of
farming to the Peak, they were also the first real
builders. At places where there were no natural
caves or fissures in the rock to inter their dead, they
constructed megalithic (simply 'big stone')
chambered tombs for them, out of solid slabs of
limestone. At least nine of these Neolithic
chambered tombs, which were used as communal
burial centres, have been identified in the White
Peak area, which appears to have been more
attractive than the less fertile Dark Peak woodlands.
Possibly it was the fertility of the easily-cleared and
friable 'loess' soils of the limestone plateau which
was a deciding factor in the settlement pattern of the
period, in addition to a decline in hunting success in
the forests on the gritstone.

Minninglow, with its scraggy cupola of ancient
beeches visible from so many viewpoints in the
Peak, is the most impressively-sited of these
Neolithic tombs. Standing above the Roman road
between Buxton and Little Chester, (now on the
outskirts of Derby) the hill top carries at least four
such tombs which would once have been covered
by an extensive cairn, now disappeared. Probably
because of its prominence, Minninglow has been
the subject of generations of digging by treasure

The spindly crown of beeches on Minninglow is a prominent landmark in many White Peak views. Here it is seen from the High Peak Trail.

hunters, from passing Roman legionaries (if the finds of Roman coins and pottery made there are anything to go by) to the Victorian barrow-diggers led by the industrious Squire Thomas Bateman of Middleton-by-Youlgreave. It is still a highly atmospheric place, with one of the finest views in the Peak District from its lonely, wind-tossed summit. Bateman was one of the most important figures in nineteenth century English archaeology, and was personally responsible for digging 200 barrows in the district, described in his classic *Ten Years' Diggings in Celtic and Saxon Gravehills* (1861).

Five Wells chambered tomb above the A6 near Taddington has the distinction of being the highest site of its kind in Britain. At over 1,400 ft (425 m) on a spur of the plateau on Taddington Moor, this much-robbed but still impressive group of weathered limestone slabs has revealed much of what we know of the Neolithic period in the Peak. Even Bateman, in his enthusiastic if unscientific programme of barrow digging, devoted a whole day in 1846 to the excavation of Five Wells, and concluded that at least twelve burials had been made in the two stone burial chambers. Later, more scientific excavations of the site revealed a systematic construction which must have involved considerable organizational skill, and fragments of pottery which suggest contacts with the rest of Britain.

But the most spectacular and visible monument left by the Neolithic settlers must be the mysterious and enigmatic henge monument and stone circle of Arbor Low, on a windswept ridge 1,230 ft (374 m) above the sea between Parsley Hay and Youlgreave. Even Thomas Bateman found Arbor Low 'the most important, as well as the most uninjured, remain of the religious edifices of our barbarous forefathers'. Variously-dubbed 'the Stonehenge of the North' or a 'power centre' of a national system of ley-lines by the lunatic fringe, Arbor Low undoubtedly retains much of its Megalithic magic. Even today, as with other ritual monuments, no one can be sure why it was constructed, but modern archaeologists have estimated it could have involved up to a million man-hours of back-breaking labour over several years to transport the forty-six large prostrate slabs of limestone to form the circle within the 250 ft (76 m) diameter bank. It is virtually certain that the stones, surrounding a central 'cove' of four, once stood upright, like those of their better-known contemporaries at Stonehenge, Avebury and elsewhere. Bateman records that a very old man from Middleton remembered the stones 'standing obliquely on one end' but no one has yet proved it, and it remains a mystery.

Most modern archaeologists are agreed that the construction of such henges required great feats of organization and building skill, and they must have been important communal gathering places, perhaps at important times of the year, such as spring, midsummer and harvest. Maybe they were trading centres as well, for finds of smoothly-polished greenstone axes, made by the craftsmen of Langdale, in the Lake District or Craig Llwyd in Snowdonia, have been made nearby, and dated to this period. These beautiful axes must have made a

An astronomical power centre, or merely a Neolithic meeting place? Arbor Low, remote and mysterious, still keeps its secrets.

major contribution to the clearance of the forests, and again point to an organized and advanced trading system.

Arbor Low, and similar Neolithic henges, like the now stoneless Bull Ring near Dove Holes, remain full of unanswered questions, and in a way, it is heartening to know that in this age of high technology, we still don't know *all* the answers. Certainly, to stand on the exposed bank of Arbor Low and look down on the venerable recumbent

stones and surrounding 'low'-topped hills, gives a
sense of continuity with the past which is almost as
tangible as the rough, venerable stones themselves.
Bateman certainly felt it, for he commented that the
solitude of the place 'almost carries the observer
back through a multitude of centuries, and makes
him believe that he sees the same view and the same
state of things as existed in the days of the architects
of this once holy fane.'

Arbor Low was important for communal
gatherings for perhaps a thousand years, for
superimposed on the bank near its south-east
entrance is a large badly damaged barrow or burial
mound dated to the Bronze Age. And two fields
away, linked to the henge by a twisting ridge of
earth, stands Gib Hill, another Bronze Age barrow,
which was also built over an oval-shaped Neolithic
cairn.

Looking round the horizon from Arbor Low or
Gib Hill you can, with the aid of a map, pick out a
whole succession of place names ending in the suffix
'low' – Carder Low, Lean Low, Caskin Low, Aleck
Low, Minninglow, Ringham Low, Bee Low, Calling
Low, Ricklow, and even, to the north, the
delightfully contradictory High Low. It has been
estimated that more than seventy place-names in
this part of the Peak contain that 'low' element
which, as explained earlier, is Old English for a
mound, and usually a burial mound.

A Bronze Age collared
urn from a barrow on
Stanton Moor.

These lows, paradoxically usually sited on high
points in the landscape, are the most obvious
evidence of the next recognizable civilization in the
Peak District. In almost every case, they mark the
last resting place of one of those Bronze Age people
who inherited the communal centre of Arbor Low
from its Neolithic builders, and continued to
worship, trade, or meet there for perhaps the next
1,000 years.

None of these burial mounds is more atmospheric
than the remote and isolated tumuli of Hob Hurst's
House, 1,000 ft (304 m) up on Brampton East Moor
above Chatsworth Park. It was excavated by
Thomas Bateman one June day in 1853 when he
found a pile of burnt human bones, 'lying in the very
spot where they had been drawn together while the
embers of the funeral pyre were glowing.' The
unusual name perpetuates the local belief in the
mischievous wood elf, 'Hob i' th' Hurst,' who in a
good mood could increase milk and hay yields, or if
irritated, might make cows go dry or shatter
crockery.

Remains of a Bronze Age
hut circle at Swine Sty, on
Big Moor.

Early Bronze Age inhabitants, from around
2,000 BC, are often known as Beaker people from
the characteristic small, highly decorated vessels
found among their grave goods. A love of high
places seems to have been a feature of Bronze Age
Peaklanders, for as well as their introduction of
metal (small bronze awls, axes or knife-daggers) for
the first time, their culture expanded from the
populous, long-established limestone heartland of
the district onto the higher, more exposed gritstone
uplands to the east and west. Several theories have
been put forward for this move, the most likely
being an increase in population after about
1,750 BC, which brought pressure to bear on
existing communities, and a possible improvement
in the climate which made the uplands more inviting
to these farmers.

Whatever the reasons, there was certainly an
influx of Bronze Age people onto the gritstone
edges and the elevated, open dip slopes beyond,
especially to the east of the River Derwent. Pollen
samples taken from Leash Fen, Barbrook and
Harland Edge on these eastern moors indicate a
light woodland environment around 2,000 BC, with
fairly extensive forest clearance going on from
1,750 BC for grazing and cropping, and blanket peat
slowly advancing on to the lower slopes.

One of the finest and most complete Bronze Age
landscapes of the southern Pennines has been

identified on the eastern moors centred on the
settlement at Swine Sty, on the western bank of the
Barbrook above Curbar. Extensive remains of
settlement earthworks, field systems, stone circles,
clearance cairns and burial cairns are 'fossilized'
under the rough moor grass in a landscape so rich
in prehistory as almost to rival that of Dartmoor.
Some of these structures have been radio-carbon
dated to between 1,800 and 1,400 BC. The whole
area came into the possession of the National Park
authority in 1984, when the Government finally
agreed a purchase price between the Park and the
Severn-Trent Water Authority. The future of this
unique and precious landscape, which we are only
just beginning to understand, thankfully seems
assured.

Today, Swine Sty stands out as a lush green island
amid the encircling bracken of the moor, enclosed

The Nine Ladies stone
circle, a Bronze Age
ceremonial monument on
Stanton Moor.

by a stone bank on three sides and a steep, natural escarpment to the north. Within the three quarters of an acre enclosure, evidence has been found of a thriving shale jewellery industry, and over sixty pieces of stone worked into bracelets and rings have been discovered. A picture emerges of a hard-working, close-knit community thriving at just below the 1,000 foot contour, gradually clearing fields from the surrounding woodland, leaving the cleared gritstone boulders piled up in well-defined cairns. Most of the farming in the Barbrook valley appears to have been pastoral, although there is some evidence of cultivation of cereals with the discovery of saddle querns, used to grind grain. While field clearance and herding took place on the dip slopes as far as the wetter ground below the next outcrops to the east, the eastern bank of the Barbrook was used as a burial ground for the occupants of Swine Sty, an ancient name which might possibly give a clue to the type of animal herded there.

Just across the Derwent valley on the isolated gritstone 'island' of Stanton Moor, standing proud and aloof from the surrounding grey-green limestone, an even more important Bronze Age necropolis existed. Here, now almost entirely hidden beneath the encroaching heather and invading silver birch, more than seventy Bronze Age burial mounds have been identified, together with ring cairns and the Nine Ladies stone circle.

'Stanton Moor', wrote H J Massingham in *The Heritage of Man*, 'is as thick with tumuli as a plumduff with raisins'. We know so much of the people to whom this place was sacred largely through the single-minded and dedicated investigation over two generations by the Heathcote family, who kept a private museum in the nearby village of Birchover for many years. For nearly thirty years, Mr J C and Mr J P Heathcote, father and son, conducted a systematic survey of the barrow-dotted surface of the moor, and became its unofficial custodians. Among the grave-goods they found were flint arrow heads, knives and scrapers, scraps of melted bronze and segmented bone beads. One small, star-shaped bead made of red 'faience' porcelain may even have originated in fourteenth century BC Egypt. But nearly all the Stanton Moor burials were cremations leaving minimal evidence behind, and most of the burial cairns had been used over and over again. A more recent study showed that twenty-one of the excavated barrows had produced evidence of no fewer than eighty-eight cremated bodies. Forest clearance was going on here too, as pollen analysis from beneath one of the ring cairns which were some kind of ceremonial structure, has shown. Heather seeds and the seeds of weeds and two types of cultivated cereals show that arable agriculture had arrived in the area by this time.

Stanton Moor must have been a sacred place of ritual from around 1,800 to at least 1,400 BC and many of these rituals must have centred around the nearby stone circle known as the Nine Ladies, with its accompanying single standing stone, the King Stone. The association of an isolated 'pointer' stone some distance from a circle is a common occurrence, matched by the King Stone associated with the Rollright Stones on the Oxfordshire/Warwickshire border, and Long Meg who stands beside her Daughters, at Salkeld in Cumbria on the edge of the Lake District. Thankfully, the completely incongruous and unnecessary stone walls which used to surround the circle and the King Stone have recently been removed, and the site, surrounded by spindly whispering birches, has regained much of its ancient, timeless mystery.

The Bronze Age proper, lasting perhaps from 2,100 to 650 BC moved slowly and imperceptibly into the period archaeologists call the Iron Age. The most tangible evidence of the 700 years of Iron Age Britain in the Peak District is the string of so-called hillforts which may have marked the southern frontier of Brigantia. It is one of the oddest unexplained facts of the Peak's prehistory, and that of most parts of Britain, that very little else, in the way of burials or artefacts, has been discovered from this period. All that these vigorous, well-organized and independent people have left us here are the huge, bank-and-ditched structures which in every case occupy a high promontory with breathtaking and extensive views in all directions.

The term 'hillfort' is now being questioned by archaeologists because it over-simplifies the functions of these airy enclosures. It was easy, before any serious and scientific investigations had been carried out on them, to classify these strategically placed centres as purely defensive sites erected in defiance of the Roman overlords. That interpretation has been updated by the detailed and careful excavations of a number of such sites, which indicate that some housed permanent settlements over a long period of time, from the later Bronze Age through to the Roman occupation and even into the troubled and confused years after the Roman withdrawal. They could have been centres for the management of summer grazing over the large areas of pasturage visible from their high ramparts, and occupied as seasonal 'shielings' by tribes who may have spent their winters on more permanent – and as yet undiscovered – settlements on the limestone plateau. The commanding position of these 'hill-forts' meant they could also have been used as look-outs over large areas of the cleared and cultivated areas of the lower limestone, and they might also have been redistribution centres for the produce of the surrounding land.

Easily the most impressive, and accessible, of these encampments is that which occupies the magnificent 1,695 ft (517 m) summit of Mam Tor which effectively blocks the end of the broad, shale Hope Valley near Castleton. Mam Tor – the name is thought to mean 'Mother Mountain' – is the most visually impressive hillfort of the southern Pennines, and at sixteen acres, the largest hillfort in the Peak. It stands at the end of the Lose Hill–Back Tor ridge of unstable shales which acts as a natural border between the White and Dark Peaks. It is hard to

Plan of the Mam Tor hillfort.

Mam Tor, perhaps the Mother Mountain of the Brigantes, dominates the Hope Valley and the village of Castleton.

imagine a better site on which to erect a centre
which could control vast areas of countryside, and
the excavations by Manchester University students
in the mid-sixties revealed that this bald hilltop may
have supported a sizeable population in the
numerous hut circles which were investigated.

They are perhaps best seen today from the air,
especially after the first light snows of winter have
dusted the top of Mam Tor. Then these hut sites
stand out like a rash of pock-marked dimples on the
bank-enclosed summit. On the eastern side of the
summit, where Mam Tor lives up to its local name of
'the Shivering Mountain', the impressive rampart
and ditch which surrounded the settlement links
with the natural defence of the landslip.

Pottery sherds found within the hut circles were
very roughly made of gritty material, dated to 1,000
to 800 BC, while fragments of a socketed bronze axe
date to around 650 BC. Charcoal samples have been
radio-carbon dated to the late Bronze Age, proving
a very early and lengthy period of occupation. As in
most of the other northern hillforts, a life-giving
spring is still to be found within Mam Tor's ramparts
– if you know where to look for it.

Other hillforts or encampments in the Peak dated
to the late Bronze Age and Iron Age include the
small promontory fortlet of Ball Cross, which

Pony trekkers on the
ancient ridgeway from
Lose Hill approach the
ramparts of Mam Tor.

overlooks Bakewell's golf course and the Wye Valley on Calton Pastures east of Bakewell, and Castle Naze overlooking Coombs and Chapel-en-le-Frith on Black Edge north of Buxton. The broodingly impressive fort of Carl Wark, east of Hathersage, most probably had its origin in the Iron Age, but the advanced methods of construction of its boulder-revetted ramparts are unlike any others in the Peak District.

Strangely, only one of these enigmatic Iron Age hillforts has been identified on the limestone, that is on the conspicuous headland of Fin Cop, which forms the impressive backdrop to so many sightseer's snap-shots of Monsal Dale from Monsal Head. Unfortunately, the interior of Fin Cop fort, like so much else on the limestone plateau, has been levelled by modern ploughing, but it may have included some kind of stock enclosures, as well as an earlier barrow.

Certainly, these extensive 'encampments' seem to have occupied a key and central role in the administration of Iron Age Peakland for hundreds of years, and for the next major development, we must return to the most spectacular of them all, Mam Tor.

The view from the ramparts looks down the hawthorn-hedged Hope Valley, beyond medieval Castleton and Hope, with the prominent white chimney of its cement works. On a low green hill at Brough, at the confluence of the River Noe with Peakshole Water, is the relatively insignificant site of the only major settlement left by the might of Imperial Rome in this wild backwater of their empire. This was the fort of Navio, a small (two-acre) site which was probably the central military control point of the extensive Roman lead mining interests in the Peak. A garrison of perhaps 500 men occupied Navio, in what must have been fairly cramped conditions, from the last quarter of the first century AD.

The wild regions of the north, including the Peak, were some time behind the south of England in being colonized by the invaders from the Mediterranean. The Roman occupation of the Peak is thought to have started around 70 AD with military incursions into the tribal territories of the Brigantes, north of the Trent. Perhaps the Roman generals had heard tales of the rich mineral wealth of the Peak, particularly its easily accessible lead veins, and determined with typical deliberation, to take what they could. Lead was almost as important a commodity as gold in those days, and a key

Solitary sessile oak, near the Snake Road, Woodlands Valley. When the Romans passed this way, the landscape was much more heavily forested with native trees like this.

indicator of imperial wealth.

Now, for the first time, we can give a name to the people who occupied the Peak, for the first written accounts of the area were left to us by the Roman conquerors. The Roman writer Tacitus claimed that the tribe known as the Brigantes were the most populous people in Britain. The homeland of this loose confederation of tribes was in the north, particularly in the hills of the Pennines, and their centres included the huge hillfort of Almondbury, overlooking modern Huddersfield.

The roads of the all-conquering Romans started to snake northwards from the regional base at Little Chester, and into the brooding and threatening hill country of the Peak. We know that the Peak was one of the most important sources of lead for the Romans in Britain because of the frequent discoveries of ingots (pigs) of the metal which have been made locally, bearing the inscription 'Lutudarum'. This must have been the Roman lead mining centre in the Peak, but it has never been positively identified. Nearly all the pigs of lead bearing this inscription have been found in the vicinity of Matlock, while many people believe the Saxon settlement of Wirksworth, important for its lead mining for centuries, may cover the Roman site of Lutudarum. On the other hand, the name might just as easily refer to the region, and not a specific centre.

Wherever Lutudarum was, it had to be defended, and Navio was occupied for perhaps two centuries, with various re-buildings and modifications in stone and timber as evidence of its continuing importance. We may never know if the fort was attacked by the native Brigantes during its early period of occupation, but the development of a 'vicus' or civilian settlement around the fort in the second and third centuries AD, seems to suggest a peaceful local dependence on the Roman fort.

The Romans are perhaps best remembered for their extensive and coherent network of often ruler-straight roads, which were the essential communication arteries which held their empire together. But again, there are many mysterious and unexplained gaps in the Roman road network of the Peak. Some routes are still quite obvious on the ground, for example the one followed for part of its way by the modern A515 Ashbourne–Buxton road, up and over the limestone plateau. This road, known in part as the Portway, linked Buxton with Little Chester.

Buxton was obviously an important centre for the

spa-seeking Romans, who knew it as Aquae Arnemetiae and were attracted by the warm springs near the head of the Wye. The road from Buxton to Navio crosses Bradwell Moor and is still known as Batham Gate, and striking evidence of this was found in the 1860s when a milestone bearing the inscription 'From Anavio Ten miles' was found at Buxton. Another Roman road linked the forts of Navio and Melandra (more correctly Ardotalia) between Glossop and Hollingworth at the foot of Longdendale, and this perhaps remains a well defined and visible route for much of its distance. In fact, Doctor's Gate, (the road takes its name from Dr John Talbot, vicar of Glossop from 1494 to 1550) built of gritstone slabs with stone kerbs still standing above the paved way, in places may not be Roman at all, but a medieval route. It climbs up the side of the Shelf Brook from Old Glossop before striking boldly into the peat cloughs and hags between Kinder Scout and Bleaklow to emerge down Lady Clough on the line of the modern Snake Road, made a turnpike in the early nineteenth century. It then skirted the eastern ramparts of Kinder Scout under Crookstone Hill and across the narrow neck of land between the valleys of the Noe and Ashop via Hope Cross, before descending into the Hope Valley through Aston.

Other Roman roads must have adapted existing well-established prehistoric trackways for some routes.

There are still many mysteries about Roman Peakland, but recent discoveries seem to indicate a settled population, engaged in peaceful farming and mining activities – the traditional dual economy of the area for at least the last 2,000 years. Occasionally faintly visible earthworks can be seen in the fading light of evening or from the air, evidence of the Romano-British settlement. But this forms the next part of our tale, as the story of the human occupation of the Peak continues to unfold.

These paved slabs on Doctor's Gate, over a shoulder of Bleaklow, are now thought to be a medieval 'improvement' to a Roman road.

3 **Between Romans and Normans**

Early summer is a busy time at Roystone Grange Farm, which shelters in a typical, crag-rimmed dry dale in the south of the limestone White Peak.

It is the time for the annual 'clip' or shearing of the sheep, and the galvanized steel sheep pens by the chapel-like, disused eighteenth-century pumping house are filled with a seething, curly-coated mass of milling animals. Occasionally, the sheep spill out over a square of large, prostrate lichen-encrusted boulders next to the metal holding pens, scraping their black hooves on the old grey stones, and filling the valley with their protesting cries.

A picturesque scene to the passing walker, but one which graphically illustrates the incredible continuity of farming life in the Peak. For almost exactly the same scene could have been witnessed nearly 2,000 years ago in exactly the same place. Those massive old boulders are in fact the foundations of a Romano-British sheep pen, and further up the valley beyond the present eighteenth/nineteenth century farmhouse, the remains of a second or third century Romano-British farm have been found. Nor was this the only settlement in this seemingly remote and isolated White Peak backwater. An impressive low-walled thatched house stood close to the farmyard, and at least four other smaller farms have been located around the hillsides to the south, indicating a population of at least fifty people, compared with perhaps ten today. Further south down the valley, opposite the shattered pine-topped limestone crags towards Ballidon, the ghostly low banks of a Roman field or allotment system can be made out by the observant eye in the fading light of day.

The valley of Roystone Grange has obviously harboured a vigorous farming community for a long time, and the nearby Neolithic chambered tomb of Minninglow and at least twelve Bronze Age barrows on the surrounding hills indicate that people have known this 'secret' valley for perhaps 5,000 years. Long after the Romano-British farmers had gone, white-robed Cistercian monks from far-off Garendon Abbey in Leicestershire developed the

Perhaps more than any other animal, sheep have shaped the Peak landscape. This Mule ewe has twin lambs.

farmstead, then known as 'Revestones', during the
Middle Ages and gave it the eponymous name of
'grange' – a monastic farm. The remains of their
substantial medieval manor house and dairy have
also been excavated just above the site of the sheep
pens. Later still, in another illustration of the
amazing succession of life in this small corner of the
Peak, a medieval village was created, thrived and
then declined down the valley near Ballidon. It is
marked today only by a tiny, isolated Norman
chapel, and the bumps and hollows of the village's
long-deserted crofts and tofts, and the corduroy
corrugations of its ridge-and-furrowed open fields.
Lead may have been worked here since Roman
times, and there is plentiful evidence of its
exploitation in the abandoned lines of the 'rakes'
across many fields.

The early nineteenth-century Cromford and High
Peak Railway – now the High Peak Trail – brought
the first hints of Industrial Revolution to the area and
Victorian lime kilns and silica brick works along its
winding, embanked route made the Roystone area a
small-scale hive of industry. That industry was
nothing in comparison with the huge modern
limestone quarry which occupies the southern end
of the valley.

As Dr Jonathan Wager of Manchester University
has observed: 'The historic landscape significance
of Ballidon lies in the remarkable preservation of
successive periods of settlement and activity.' But
Ballidon and its associated community at Roystone

Walkers and cyclists
approach Minninglow on
the High Peak Trail.

Grange is by no means unusual in this part of the Peak. 'Everything', as Professor W G Hoskins, the 'father' of English landscape history rightly observed, 'is older than we think'. And Dr Wager, in his seminal report on the conservation of historic landscapes in the national park, pointed out: 'Much of the history of the Peak District is not recorded in documents, but is locked away in the landscape of the Park.' Few places in Britain have a more fascinating and continuous story to tell, and few places reward the diligent landscape detective so richly as the hills and dales of the Peak.

Roystone's Romano-British farming settlement has become an exciting example of 'public archaeology', for its 5,000 years of history is interpreted by a popular four-mile trail in which modern visitors are taken on a fascinating time-trip back into Peakland history. It is one of the most recently investigated settlements of the Romano-British period, incidentally made possible only through the interested and enlightened attitude of the modern farmer and the enthusiasm of another from a neighbouring parish, co-operating with archaeologists from Sheffield University. But it is by no means the only one so far discovered in the dales of the White Peak. By the time of the Romans, the landscape of the area was obviously well settled and 'civilized' into numerous small settlements.

West of Millers Dale, on the latest of the National Park's converted railway trails, the Monsal Trail (which follows the line of the former Midland Railway), the River Wye takes a sweeping bend to the north before returning to its easterly course. The deflection is marked by the sheer 300 ft (91 m) wall of naked limestone known as Chee Tor, which rises out of the ashwoods of the dale and is the site of some of the most severe rock climbs in the Peak. On the gently sloping promontory above the rushing river, a series of low banks in the short, sheep-cropped turf mark the foundations of another Romano-British settlement. These faint remains are best seen in the dying daylight or under snow from the road up to Wormhill from Millers Dale, on the opposite side of the river. They have been dated to the third and fourth centuries from the sherds of pottery and a single burial which have been found. These rectangular plots are often misleadingly marked on maps as 'Celtic Fields', but in fact can sometimes be Roman or prehistoric in origin, and need not be associated with Celtic farmers.

On the Chee Tor site, they cover about twenty-

Looking down on the Monsal Dale viaduct, once part of the Midland line and now part of the Monsal Trail. In the background is Upperdale.

five acres, and nearby the unmistakable 'giant's staircase' of medieval strip lynchets can be seen marching up the steeper slopes. These are cultivation terraces, produced by ploughing teams of oxen contouring across the slopes after all the flatter land had been used. Now they are crossed by eighteenth-century enclosure walls, evidence again of continuous cultivation over perhaps 2,000 years.

Nearly forty Romano-British settlements have been discovered in the White Peak, and surveys by Dr Richard Hodges of Sheffield University and Mr Martin Wildgoose of Kniveton around Roystone Grange have shown that some of their field walls are, incredibly, still in use. The large, lichen-covered boulders which often form the base stones of later medieval and eighteenth- and nineteenth-century drystone walls have proved by excavation to have been erected in the second century AD. These 'orthostats', or bulky stones, first marked out the estates of Romano-British farms and settlements and later had the neater, roughly-hewn stones of the enclosure movement walls (which local tradition says were built by the forced labour of Napoleonic prisoners of war) superimposed upon them.

The Roman farming unit at Roystone appears to have been laid out by these orthostat walls into a huge 'butterfly' shape, with one 'wing' devoted to winter pasture, and the other to arable farming, with the farmhouse at the centre and open summer pasture beyond the encompassing walls.

As the four centuries of Roman domination slowly came to a close, and the legionaries and auxiliaries stationed to control the Empire's lead mining interests at Navio were finally withdrawn perhaps for the defence of Rome, we enter that little-understood period which historians call 'The Dark Ages'.

Water's edge view of the Dove in Dovedale.

Although year by year we are discovering that the Dark Ages were not so 'dark', at least in terms of artistic achievement, as the history books used to claim, our knowledge of the next thousand years of Peak District history is still very indistinct. Apart from a handful of documents, chronicles and surveys and a few meagre artefacts in the form of carved stones and burials, the most common evidence of this important transitional period in the Peak landscape is found in that most enduring aspect of our heritage – place-names. We have to revert to the local oral tradition, perpetuated in place-names, to recognize when and where settlements took place in those confused and

Only in winter does the River Dove, seen here in Wolfscote Dale, live up to its British name which meant 'dark'.

confusing years which followed the departure of the Roman legions.

Indeed, some of our more prominent landscape features seem to have been given British names long before the Anglian and Danish newcomers filtered up the dales and river valleys from the south, east and west. Rivers, in particular, have names which may have been in everyday use for perhaps two thousand years. These include the Derwent, which is derived from the British 'derva' meaning oak, and thus is equivalent to 'the river where oaks are common', the Dove, derived from the British 'dubo' meaning 'black' or 'dark', and the Noe, which simply means 'to flow'.

The common Peak District suffix of 'tor' is also thought to have Celtic origins, and was adopted by the English settlers as the local name for a rocky hill or high rock, although why it is only found here in the southern tip of the Pennines and in the West Country is unexplained. The prominent and commanding hill of Mam Tor, which overlooks the length of the Hope Valley, has obviously been a place of importance since prehistory, as the Bronze and Iron Age hillfort round its summit signifies. The

Pagoda Rocks, near Edale Head on the Kinder Scout plateau. The name 'Kinder Scout' is thought to refer to the hundred-foot waterfall of Kinder Downfall.

'mam' element comes perhaps from another ancient British word, corresponding with a Welsh word meaning 'mother' and an Irish word meaning 'breast'. It is therefore not too much of a presumption, bearing in mind the long-standing strategic importance of this shapely, rounded hill, to suggest that it may have been known to local people as 'The Mother Mountain' since the Iron Age. There is also a strong local tradition that the periodic landslips on its east face constantly 'give birth' to smaller hills, including one known as 'Little Mam Tor', on the slopes below. The highest mountain in the Peak, Kinder Scout, also contains an ancient British prefix, together with the descriptive Old Norse 'skuti', meaning a high, overhanging rock.

The earliest English documentary record of the name of the Peak and its inhabitants comes in the dry text of The Tribal Hidage, a seventh-century tribute list drawn up to assess the taxable value of the Anglian kingdom of Mercia and its dependents. From this, we learn that the Pecsaetan, or 'dwellers of the Peak', held lands amounting to 1,200 'hides'. A hide was a unit of land equivalent to that needed to support one household (later reckoned to be about 120 acres or 48 hectares), so we can guess that the area could have supported about 1,200 families, probably descendants of those Romano-British farmers who first 'civilized' the area.

But 'Mercia' itself means 'borderland', and the hills and dales of the Peak must again have marked a tenuous frontier zone, this time between the powerful Saxon kingdom of Mercia, Celtic Elmet and Northumbria. Here and there, traces and echoes of those pagan days can be found in the Peak, and place-names again provide the most lasting evidence. Before Mercia's conversion to Christianity in the middle of the seventh century, the Pecsaetan still may have worshipped the old, pagan gods which had probably been deified since the days of prehistory.

Wensley, and its associated dry valley of Wensleydale, in the south-east corner of the national park east of Winster, is thought to get its name from Woden, the Scandinavian god of war. The name incorporates the Old English term 'leah', meaning a clearing in a wood, so the name of this now-peaceful hamlet means 'Woden's clearing'. Five miles away and high on the bleak limestone plateau, the settlement of Friden with its refractory brickworks alongside the former Cromford and High Peak Railway, may celebrate a heathen Germanic goddess, Frīg, or Frija, the Earth Mother, who also gave her name to Friday.

But the most graphic indication of the coming of Christianity to the pagan tribes of the Peak was uncovered one May morning in 1848 by that extraordinary Victorian barrow-digger Thomas Bateman, on a high and exposed hill just east of the Ashbourne–Buxton road 'near the eighth milestone from the latter place'.

Bateman seems instantly to have recognized the importance of his excavations at Benty Grange, the name of the nearby farm. 'It was our good fortune to open a barrow which afforded a more instructive collection of relics than has ever been discovered in the county, and which are not surpassed in interest by any remains hitherto recovered from any Anglo-Saxon burying place in the kingdom' he enthuses in *Ten Years' Diggings*. Over a century after his breathless account, the Benty Grange remains are still unique in Europe, marking a princely burial dated to the latter half of the seventh century, just as the light of Christianity began to illuminate the so-called 'Dark Ages'.

The Pecsaetan warrior who was buried at Benty Grange reflects the uncertainty of the times, for in a sense the personal effects buried with him indicated he was hedging his spiritual bets. The most famous artefact from the barrow was a magnificent iron helmet, now in Weston Park Museum, Sheffield. The important thing about the Benty Grange helmet to the historian is that it features an intriguing mixture of both pagan and Christian motifs in its decoration. On its crest is the unmistakable form of a crouching boar, with eyes of garnets set in gold and decorated with silver studs and plates. Bateman realized the

The Benty Grange helmet provides a unique link between the pagan Dark Ages and the coming of Christianity in the Peak.

savage significance of the boar (an animal sacred to Frīg incidentally, remembered at nearby Friden) and recalled mention of boar-decorated helmets in Beowulf, 'The hog of gold, the boar hard as iron'.

But the nose-piece of the corroded helmet was ornamented by a Latin cross in silver, and it is the combination of this Christian symbol, together with three hanging bowl escutcheons and a silver-decorated leather drinking cup, with the pagan symbol of the boar and method of burial, which makes the Benty Grange burial so significant.

The Peak was certainly on the periphery of Mercian power, perhaps a border-zone as already suggested, and it is only here and there from the evidence of place-names that we can make any guesses as to the extent of Anglian settlement in the area. It is thought that this period saw the first rise to prominence of the place which is now generally regarded as the 'capital' of the Peak District, Bakewell.

Bakewell contains the 'well' element which is thought to have evolved from the Old English word 'waelle' meaning a spring or stream. So Bakewell means 'Badeca's spring' and perhaps perpetuates the name of the Anglian lord who inherited the area from the first settlers of Ball Cross. Other villages which use this Old English Midland dialect word in their names include Tideswell – 'Tidi's spring' – and Bradwell, which probably means 'broad stream'.

But there is also more tangible and visible evidence for Bakewell's growing importance in those dark days, apart from its name. The hilltop church site of All Saints, overlooking the broad valley of the Wye and the wooded crest of Calton Pastures beyond, is thought to be very ancient. Nikolaus Pevsner thought that the masonry at the west end of the nave of the heavily-restored parish church might include part of the original Saxon building on the site, and certainly the many fragments of carved stones collected in the south porch date from those times.

But the greatest Saxon treasure of Bakewell is to be found behind some iron railings in the churchyard. It is the mutilated but still magnificent Saxon cross shaft, which has been dated to the end of the eighth century, when Mercia was at the height of its power and influence. The eight-foot high cross shaft is blackened and chipped with age, but still exhibits the vigour of its Saxon creator. Its panels illustrate the Christian themes of the Crucifixion and the Annunciation and the deeply-incised spiral

Above Twelve hundred years after its creation, the Saxon cross in Bakewell churchyard still exhibits the power of its sculptor.

Opposite All Saints parish church, Bakewell, seen here from Yeld Road, probably stands on the site of a Saxon church or monastery.

patterns and vine-scrolls also hide an archer holding a short bow. This is not the cross's original position; it was brought into the churchyard from a site out in the country, where it was probably used as a wayside preaching cross. A smaller tenth-century cross stump, also highly-decorated, stands outside the south porch of the church, and was brought to Bakewell from near Gladwin's Mark, on Harewood Moor east of Beeley.

The abundance and richness of Saxon carved stones in the Bakewell area could indicate that a school of Saxon sculptors was based in the vicinity of the town, perhaps at the 'coenubium', or monastery, mentioned in a charter of 949. Perhaps they were also responsible for the truncated weathered gritstone cross which stands in Eyam churchyard, the uppermost section of whose shaft is unfortunately missing, although the head remains. The cross lay neglected in a corner of the churchyard as late as the eighteenth century, when prison reformer John Howard restored it to its present position. In the early twentieth century, one of the pleasures of village children was apparently to climb up and sit on its arms. The Eyam cross, with its strongly carved vine scrolls, knotwork and carving of the Virgin and Child on its shaft, was thought by Pevsner to show influences of the Northumbrian school of sculpture. Local tradition says the cross originally stood on Eyam Moor, where perhaps missionaries from Iona or Lindisfarne first preached the Gospel in Peakland.

Other decorated cross shafts from the Anglo-Scandinavian period can be seen at Hope, Ilam, Alstonefield and at Cleulow, where the cross is probably still in its original position in a scraggy plantation of wind-tossed trees off the Congleton road above Wincle.

The truncated Saxon cross in Eyam churchyard might have been the work of the Bakewell school of craftsmen.

More than thirty of these preaching crosses survive in the Peak District, making it the most important centre of Anglo-Saxon sculpture outside Durham. Yet little is done to protect or preserve these thousand-year-old works of art, and they are left outside to face the elements, including today, the ravages of acid rain. One wonders what the outcry would be if a Turner or Constable painting was subjected to the same treatment!

Bakewell was the scene, in 920 AD, of one of the most important events in Anglo-Saxon history, when Edward the Elder, son of Alfred the Great, called a great council to unite the kingdom. We are told in the Anglo-Saxon Chronicle that he travelled up from

The shaft of Cleulow cross lies hidden in the beeches in the middle distance, and is echoed by the modern sentinel of the Macclesfield Forest post-office tower, on the right.

Wessex and took Nottingham, before moving into the Peak. He ordered a 'burh', or fortified place, to be built in the vicinity of Bakewell and manned by his ealdormen.

Here, in his fortress by the Wye (yet to be positively identified) Edward called the warring factions of the Scots, Northumbrians, English, Danes, Norse and 'Strathclyde Welsh' round the table in a great summit of unification. The result, no doubt after much debate and feasting, was that Edward was chosen as 'father and lord' by all those present, and arguably became the first monarch of all Britain.

The following year, Edward died and his son, Athelstan, born in Wessex but king of Mercia, further united the Saxon kingdoms and granted charters in 926 at Bakewell, Hope and Ashford, a grouping of estates which seem to indicate a single, wealthy region, perhaps based on lead mining which was still intact when Domesday Book was compiled in 1086. Other charters were granted at Stanton-in-the-Peak in 968; Aston in 926 and Parwich in 966, showing the area to be favoured by those early English kings to honour their loyal supporters.

Most history books regard the period from about 830 on, as the period when Viking invaders in their fearsome longboats, began to harrass, pillage and rape Britain. But again, there is not much evidence of such melodramatic events in the Peak, although the region must have been on the borders between the Danelaw to the east, and the areas of Viking Norse incursions to the north-west. It is a pattern borne out by place-names, although Scandinavian elements are thin on the ground. Only Thorpe, at the southern end of Dovedale, and Rowland, a hamlet nestling under Longstone Edge, can be directly attributed to Scandinavian sources, although the scatter of 'hulme' place names (Kettleshulme and Hulme End) in the south west of the Park may also come from the Danish 'hulm' meaning an island or a water meadow. The decorated stones and cross shafts, previously mentioned, left more lasting and tangible evidence of the vigorous art of the Viking era.

But interestingly, Derbyshire, which takes its name from Derby (a Scandinavian name perhaps meaning 'the settlement where deer were seen') was one of the areas of the Danelaw, and the county town (formerly Northworthy) was the headquarters of the Danish army in the tenth century. In the Domesday Book, Derbyshire was divided into the Danish 'wapentakes', in contrast to the 'hundreds' of Anglo-Saxon Wessex, adopted by neighbouring Cheshire and Staffordshire. These westerly counties also used the Saxon 'hides' and 'virgates' as the basis of assessment of the worth of the land, whereas Derbyshire's wealth is assessed in the characteristic Danish units of 'carucates' and 'bovates'. Derbyshire was never 'decimalised' either, like the counties to the south and west. Tax assessments were made Danish-fashion, in units of three, six or twelve, instead of in tens as elsewhere, so it can be safely assumed that pre-Domesday, administration was based on the Scandinavian model.

But what of the actual, physical evidence of this mysterious, yet obviously important period of the Peak's history? Sadly, despite the rich sepulchral,

The Bar Dyke, a mysterious Dark Age earthwork probably marking a territorial boundary on Broomhead Moor.

sculptural and documentary evidence and tantalising place-name clues, there is little archaeological proof of its passing. Except, that is, for two enigmatic earthworks which no one has satisfactorily explained, but which could well date from the Dark Age divisions and power-struggles.

The first, the Bar Dyke is a heather-clad embankment which spans the ridge between the valleys of the Ewden Beck and Hobson Moss Dike, on Broomhead Moor. Its origin is still a mystery, although local legends relate the tale of a bitter battle fought on these heights above the Don valley.

The other, known as the Grey Ditch, crosses the valley of the Bradwell Brook, just north of Bradwell, between Mich Low and Rebellion Knoll, and bisects the Roman road, Batham Gate, as it approaches Navio. The strategic nature of this hawthorn-studded rampart and ditch seems irrefutable but when it was built and by whom, no one can say. Most probably, these embankments marked territorial divisions between tribes or families, like the more famous and contemporary Offa's Dyke which marked the boundary between England and Wales.

The mysterious Grey Ditch stands within sight of the huge bulk of Win Hill across the broad, green Hope Valley. A persistent local legend explains the name of Win Hill and its shapely sister peak of Lose Hill, across the valley of the Noe, in terms of the winners and losers of an undocumented battle of about this period. Edwin, king of Northumbria marched south in pursuit of Cuicholm, king of Wessex, who had plotted an unsuccessful assassination attempt on Edwin, in which the Northumbrian's thane, Lilla, was murdered instead. The two armies met in the Peak, and camped on the two hills opposite each other, with the rushing waters of the Noe between.

The following day, the battle was joined, and Edwin emerged victorious after the ferocious encounter in which the Noe's waters were said to have run red from the blood of the slain. Needless to say, Edwin had camped on 'Win' Hill, and the loser, Cuicholm, on 'Lose' Hill – and the names remain as reminders of that long-forgotten clash of the Dark Ages.

4 **The landscape of settlement**

Two of the most tantalizing words in Domesday Book, the monumental survey commissioned by William of Normandy twenty years after his conquest of England, are 'wasta est', meaning 'it is waste'.

They are applied to nearly fifty manors in the Peak District, suggesting at first sight a worthless wilderness stretching north from the Upper Dove along the western side of the Peak to Axe Edge, the Cheshire fringe, and encompassing no fewer than a dozen 'vills' or villages in Longdendale. But historians have argued for years about what exactly that taciturn Latin phrase might mean. Explanations range from a calculated, heartless act of genocide by the Conqueror, to a peaceful movement away from the always-marginal settlements in the hills to the more easily-worked farmsteads and manors of the lowlands to the west and east.

Both these extreme solutions have been argued

The railway, power lines and a major trunk road have brought a different kind of wasteland to modern Longdendale.

for the Peak's 'wastelands', and as usual, the truth probably lies somewhere in between. Certainly we know that after the rebellions against the Norman overlords in 1069–70, William sent considerable forces into the North Country to subjugate his new kingdom. This 'Harrying of the North' took place against the background of the murder of two of the King's earls as they attempted to enter Northumbria, and the landing in the Humber of a Danish army in support of the insurgents. Some estimates put the total number of people killed in these uprisings as high as 100,000, and certainly many villages seem to have been put to the fire and sword and forcibly depopulated at this time, as a comparison with Saxon and Norman values in Domesday appears to indicate. Maybe some of the Peak's isolated hill villages, ideal in their mountain fastnesses as hideouts for fleeing rebels, suffered in this way. The Domesday entry for Longdendale records twelve manors, including Hayfield, Glossop and Kinder ('Chendre'), with the curt remark: 'All Longdendale is waste; woodland, unpastured, fit for hunting.' The value before the Conquest was put at the relatively high figure of forty shillings, with no figure at all for 1086.

But mention of the fact that this important cross-Pennine valley was only 'fit for hunting' might give a possible clue to its sudden depopulation. For Longdendale and the River Etherow marked the northern boundary of the Royal Forest of the Peak, which covered about forty square miles and was administered purely so that medieval kings could enjoy the pleasures of the hunt. The boundaries of the Peak's Royal Forest, as defined in 1305, followed the Goyt and Etherow to the west and north, then crossed the head of the Derwent before following it south and turning west to the foot of Bradwell Dale. They reached the Wye south of Tideswell, an important administrative centre of the forest where Edward I stayed for three days while hunting in 1275.

The planned medieval township of Castleton, seen from Peveril Castle.

A rare insight into the success of that visit is given in an order issued to Roger Lestrange, bailiff of the Peak, in August of that year, in which he was instructed that 'all the venison in the King's larder at Tydeswell be taken and carried to Westminster to be delivered to the keeper of the King's larder there'. One suspects that the venison would have reached an advanced state of maturity after its 150 mile journey! The Royal Forest of the Peak, not an area of vast tree cover but merely open hunting

This view of Peveril Castle, from Cave Dale, cannot have changed much since the days when it was the administrative headquarters of the Royal Forest of the Peak.

country, was to be one of the most important landscape features of the Peak for the next 500 years, before its official 'disafforestation' after complaints of 'the severity, trouble and vigour of the forest laws' in 1674.

Other animals hunted in the Royal Forest of the Peak must have included wolves, wild boar, wild cat, and both the native red and Norman-introduced fallow deer. Now and again, ancient place names remind us still of the quarry hunted by those royal sportsmen, for example, Wildboarclough, Wolf Edge and Wolfscote Dale, and Deer Holes on the banks of the infant Derwent. Forest laws, administered by full-time officials like Roger Lestrange, were harsh, especially in regard to the taking of game, or for clearing any of the few trees from the area – a regular occurrence in Edale and the Hope Valley, according to the records. Offenders found literally 'red-handed' with the blood of a freshly killed animal on them were charged with the crime of 'bloody hand', or 'back bear' if found carrying a dead animal across their shoulders. But although penalties could include the loss of limbs or even death, no case of capital punishment was recorded, and most offenders escaped with a fine or imprisonment.

Another royal forest, that of Macclesfield, occupied the western flank of the Pennines, and was administered by Ranulph, Earl of Chester. It is echoed today in the extensive Forestry Commission plantations of the same name on the hills above Macclesfield.

The first centre for the administration of the Royal Forest of the Peak was Peveril Castle at Castleton, the most impressive medieval landmark of the Peak, which receives its first mention in Domesday. This indicates that it was one of the earliest stone-built castles in England and gives a clue to its strategic importance. Perhaps, like the Roman fort of Navio just down the Hope Valley at Brough, Peveril Castle, in its almost impregnable position on the rocky spur between Peak Cavern and Cave Dale, was designed to overawe and subjugate the natives by its very situation.

The castle was built by William Peverel, an illegitimate son of an illegitimate father, William the Conqueror, who seems to have found favour because he was made Steward of the Royal Forest of the Peak, given lordship over a dozen manors in the district and made the King's Bailiff for three more, Bakewell, Ashford and Hope.

The Domesday entry refers to the once-common local name for the gaping void of Peak Cavern below the castle walls (the largest cave entrance in Britain), as 'Pechefers' which is translated as 'Peak's Arse'. It was still known by that unflattering name in the early eighteenth century, when those pioneer tourists, Celia Fiennes and Daniel Defoe passed this way, although the more prudish Defoe referred to it as 'the Devil's A . . e'. Arnbern and Hunding held the land where the castle stood before the Conquest, and it was worth fifty shillings in 1086, compared with only forty shillings in the days of Edward the Confessor.

Peverel built the stone curtain wall along the north side of the castle crag, overlooking the township which was built in its shadow and took its name, and you can still see this earliest work in the distinctive 'herringbone' masonry of the walls. Later in the twelfth century, these walls were extended to the west and east, but the great square tower, sixty feet in height, was not added until 1175–6 when Henry II repossessed the castle and spent £200 on works on his 'castelli de Pech'. The second William Peverel, son of the first, had fallen out of favour with the crown after he had allegedly poisoned his mistress's husband, the Earl of Chester, in 1155.

Henry II seems to have taken a liking to his castle in the Peak and was a regular visitor on hunting

The unique tradition of the Castleton Garlanding takes place every year on Oak Apple Day (May 29). The 'King' is encased in a weighty, bell-shaped garland of flowers and rides through the village, accompanied by his lady and much local merriment.

trips, as was Henry III and Edward III. In 1157, Henry II received the submission of Malcolm IV of Scotland at his 'Castellum de Pech'. It was probably under Henry's orders that Castleton, the planned medieval township nestling under the protective presence of the castle, grew up.

As you ascend the modern concrete path up to the castle from the custodian's cottage near the Market Square, the unmistakable grid-iron pattern of the planned town is revealed below. At the centre was the now partly-built-upon Market Square, with the Parish Council of St Edmund standing at one corner. The zig-zag decoration of the church's Norman chancel arch echoes exactly that of the gateway to the castle, suggesting the same architect.

If you look closely to the right of the large village car park beside the leat to the former water mill, you might discern the embankments of the Town Ditch, which encompassed the whole of Henry's planned town. It is also clearly visible from the Siggate road beyond Townhead to the east of the town (where the familiar 'reversed S' shape of medieval strip ploughing is also evident in the meadows of the former open field). On the outskirts of the town on the Hope road, the earthworks of a medieval hospital – for the sick and poor – have been traced.

But despite its favour with medieval monarchs, and its apparent importance as a centre for lead mining interests, Castleton cannot be regarded as a success, and it never expanded enough to fill the boundaries which Henry and his burgesses had set for it. By 1255, there were forty-three and five-eighths burgages (or householders) and seventy-one stall-holders in the market town, but it seems to have declined as the castle lost its importance.

Much more successful, and probably well-established by the time of Domesday, was Bakewell, referred to in William's great survey as 'Badequella'. This was land belonging to the King and it included, with the outlying settlements of Nether and Over Haddon, Holme, Rowsley, Burton, Conkesbury, One Ash and Monyash, a mill, a lead mine, two priests and a church, and a man-at-arms holding sixteen acres of land and two smallholders. A grant of a weekly market and a fifteen-day fair was formalized in 1254 to William Gernon, lord of the manor, although it is certain that Bakewell must have been a trading and marketing centre long before that, bearing in mind its importance in Saxon days. By 1066, the people of Bakewell, Ashford and Hope were donating £30, with $5\frac{1}{2}$ sesters (about 176 ounces) of honey and five cartloads of lead, each containing fifty slabs, to the King annually. But by 1086, a rent of £10 6s was being paid instead.

The mention of a man-at-arms at Bakewell is

Map showing the site and growth of Bakewell.

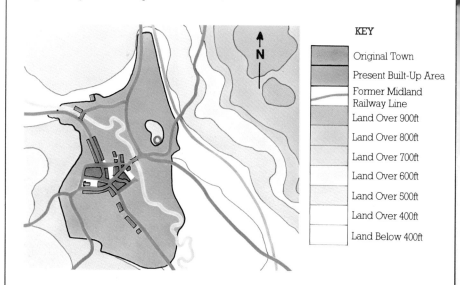

KEY

Original Town

Present Built-Up Area

Former Midland
Railway Line

Land Over 900ft

Land Over 800ft

Land Over 700ft

Land Over 600ft

Land Over 500ft

Land Over 400ft

Land Below 400ft

interesting, although there is no reference to a castle. The Domesday chroniclers did not always mention castles in their mammoth survey, probably because they were the King's property and therefore not liable to taxation. The prominent mound, or 'motte' at the eastern end of the fourteenth century town bridge has been known as Castle Hill at least since 1439, but probably dates to the late twelfth century. At one time, this conspicuously sited motte with its surrounding bailey was thought to be Edward the Elder's 'burh' mentioned in 920 in the Anglo-Saxon Chronicle, but modern research indicates that its construction was much later, perhaps dating from the civil wars of King Stephen's reign.

Dating approximately from the same period are the enigmatic earthworks of Pilsbury Castle, which stand guard over the upper reaches of the Dove valley north of Hartington. This remote and secret place, at the end of a little-used track, is recorded as 'Pilesberie' in Domesday, and the 'burh' element may indicate that the Norman builders of this, the most perfect motte and bailey castle in the Peak, may merely have been consolidating a place fortified since Saxon times.

This area on the eastern bank of the Dove is a rich one in which to explore and investigate the medieval agricultural expansion into some of the more marginal parts of the limestone plateau. Within the space of a few square miles are no fewer than five farms with the tell-tale name of 'grange',

Typical White Peak cottages at Monyash, with limestone walls, gritstone slates and dressed gritstone window surrounds.

The earthworks of Pilsbury Castle, in the Upper Dove near Hartington, are the best preserved example of a motte and bailey in the Peak District.

which usually indicates outlying farms of monasteries. In the fourteenth century, the monasteries of the Midlands and northern England were among the major suppliers to the highly-lucrative wool markets which were providing cloth for much of Britain and Europe. Great flocks of sheep roamed across the rolling 1,000 foot limestone plateau, and in the case of Cronkston Grange, between the Dove and the line of the Roman Ashbourne–Buxton road, you can still see how the original grange settlement gradually enclosed more and more of the surrounding unimproved wilderness. Huge concentric circles, now marked on the map by more modern stone walls and older earth banks and ditches, spread out from the grange site, which was associated with the Cistercian Merevale Abbey in Warwickshire, along with the adjoining granges of Pilsbury, just south of the Castle, and Needham, west of Cronkston.

The Cronkston Grange complex of banks and

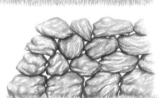

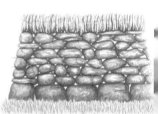

How to date Drystone walls. From top: Romano-British 'orthostats'; medieval; late medieval; enclosure walls of the eighteenth-nineteenth century.

The enclosure walls at Chelmorton 'fossilize' the ancient strip fields of the villagers, and run off at right angles to the single street.

A typical grange-type farm above Lathkill Dale, with limestone block walls and gritstone quoins and lintels.

The drystone walls of Taddington.

ditches, covering an area of more than 247 acres, has been identified as one of the finest and best preserved sites showing this important phase of farming expansion in the southern Peak. Together with the adjacent shrunken medieval village which still goes under the rather grand name of Hurdlow Town (and which also has its own grange), this landscape contrasts sharply with the intricate network of narrow enclosure fields around other villages, like Monyash and Chelmorton.

Chelmorton's famous pattern of walls, stretching back from the village street and 'fossilizing' the narrow strip fields of the medieval farmers, is a classic illustration of this type of cultivation.

In these villages and many others like Flagg and Taddington, the seventeenth- and eighteenth-century stone walls which are such a striking feature of the Peak landscape to visitors, often mark the parallel cultivation strips of the former medieval open field, and close study of the two-and-a-half inch map will even show the classic 'reversed S' shape in the narrow rectangular fields, caused by turning the eight-strong ploughing teams of oxen.

Agricultural expansion, either by those land-grabbing monks who owned nearly fifty granges in the Peak, or by the hungry and largely self-sufficient villages, extended into the Dark Peak valleys too. The disafforestation of the Royal Forest of the Peak, which had been going on piecemeal for centuries under the process known as 'assarting', allowed

Upper Booth in the Edale Valley is a settlement based on a herdsman's hut, for a 'booth' was originally a temporary shelter used by cattlemen.

pioneer farmers into areas which previously had been barred from agriculture. The Woodlands and Edale valleys, sheltering under some of the highest hills in the Peak, were occupied by farms owned by the Crown, known as 'vaccaries' and seem to have largely been used for the raising of hardy hill cattle. The string of five 'booths' – Upper Booth, Barber Booth, Grindsbrook Booth, Ollerbrook Booth and Nether Booth – marching up the Edale valley, are an echo of these medieval cattle farms, for the name comes from the Old English word meaning 'cow-house' or 'herdsman's hut'. Grindsbrook Booth is, in fact, the correct name for Edale village, in the shadow of Kinder Scout.

All this agricultural expansion, especially marked in the years before 1300, saw the creation of a number of new villages and farms, and the establishment of many new boroughs, markets and fairs, like those already mentioned at Castleton and Bakewell. Other markets and fairs are first recorded at Tideswell in 1251, Monyash in 1340 and Hartington in 1203. In the case of the bleak, grey township of Tideswell, a thousand feet up in a shallow basin of the limestone plateau, further evidence of this early medieval wealth is provided in the superb parish church, which is popularly known as 'the Cathedral of the Peak'.

Tideswell church was founded on the wealth gained from both wool and lead, and remains a rarity among English parish churches because it was entirely built in the relatively short period of fifty years from about 1320, with only a brief interruption apparently caused by the Black Death in 1348–9. Its beautifully proportioned chancel, in the late-Decorated style, with tall, traceried windows of clear glass is perhaps its greatest glory, described by one early writer as 'one gallery of light and beauty'. That continuity of construction, probably supervised by Sir John Foljambe, whose brass, dated 1383, is in the sanctuary, makes Tideswell church the most complete medieval parish church in the Peak. The eight-pinnacled west tower was the last part to be constructed, and shows the transition to the later, Perpendicular style which came into fashion towards the end of the fourteenth century.

Only Bakewell's parish church, with its possible Saxon origins, can match the splendour of Tideswell. There is some Norman work still to be seen in the west end, but most of the building seems to date from the thirteenth and fourteenth centuries, a rebuilding once again based on the wealth gained from lead and wool. Youlgreave's commanding Perpendicular-style tower of about 1400 is one of the finest in the Peak, and there is much Norman work inside, especially in the round arches of the arcaded nave. The splendid parish church of Eyam is full of reminders of the tragic 'visitation' of the Great Plague in 1665–66, when 267 villagers died in heroic self-imposed quarantine to stop the pestilence from spreading further afield. Similar plagues must, however, have struck other villages, and Tissington's well-dressing, first recorded in 1758, is said to have been revived to give thanks for deliverance from the Plague.

Many of the Peak's great land-owning families, some of which are remembered in magnificent tombs in these village churches, gained their wealth from the traditional dual-economy of the region, which was based on farming and mining. And just as this wealth created the outstanding parish churches of the area, it also gave us some of our finest medieval mansions. To make room for these opulent expressions of wealth, whole villages were sometimes moved to improve the settings of the mansions, and to gain privacy for the lords. Examples of this are the three villages of Chatsworth, Edensor and Langley which were either removed or 'transplanted' to make way for the Cavendish seat of Chatsworth, and Nether Haddon, which only survives in its beautiful twelfth-

'The Cathedral of the Peak' at Tideswell, built on the wealth gained from lead and wool.

The oak-panelled banqueting hall at Haddon, a medieval masterpiece.

and thirteenth-century chapel, now incorporated in the mainly mid-fourteenth-century manor house of Haddon Hall, on the banks of the Wye south of Bakewell.

Haddon, home of the Duke of Rutland, has often been described as one of the finest examples of a medieval great house in the country, and its time-worn courtyards and oak-panelled rooms still exude the atmosphere of the period. It owes its medieval perfection and completeness to the fact that it remained untouched and empty for about two hundred years when it was abandoned in favour of the family's other home of Belvoir Castle in Rutland. The first stronghold on the site was probably built by the same William Peverel who built Peveril Castle at Castleton, but it later passed into the Vernon family which was united with the other great local family of the Manners by the celebrated, but probably fictional, elopement of Dorothy Vernon with Sir John Manners. The disapproving father in this fanciful legend was Sir George Vernon, who inherited the estate in 1515, and was known as 'the King of the Peak' from his great autocratic power and wealth.

Chatsworth House has been the seat of the Cavendish family since the sixteenth century, and the first Tudor house was largely built by another legendary figure in Peak history, Bess of Hardwick. Elizabeth Hardwick had four husbands, each one richer than the last, and despite a spell in the Tower of London for suspected support of Mary, Queen of Scots, she became a powerful figure in Tudor England. All that remains of Bess's original Chatsworth is the turreted Hunting Tower in the woods behind the house, and the summer retreat or belvedere of Queen Mary's Bower in the grounds. Mary was actually a frequent enforced guest at Chatsworth during her long term of imprisonment.

Much of the present Palladian-fronted building dates from the rebuilding of 1687, carried out by William Cavendish, the fourth Earl, later to become the first Duke of Devonshire. William Talman was the first architect, but it has been suggested that when he fell out with the Duke after the first phase, the Duke may have designed the principal western façade of the house himself, assisted by Thomas Archer. The interior of Chatsworth is a treasure house of works of art from all over the world, and the sumptuous apartments bear out the popular nickname of the house – 'the Palace of the Peak'. The

The west front of Chatsworth, seen across the so-called 'Michelangelo Bridge' over the River Derwent.

villages of Chatsworth, Edensor and Langley (all mentioned in Domesday) disappeared under Lancelot 'Capability' Brown's landscaped parklands, and Sir Joseph Paxton's immaculate gardens.

The classic Palladian style was also adopted by the Legh family of Lyme Hall, on the far west of the Peak near Stockport, when they commissioned Leoni to rebuild their Tudor and Jacobean home in the eighteenth century. The Leghs had held Lyme since the fourteenth century, and the enclosed deer park, part moorland and part woodland, still contains a fine herd of red deer, in a habitat which closely parallels those royal medieval hunting forests.

Many smaller manors dating from the period of medieval prosperity can still be traced in the Peakland landscape today. There are examples at North Lees Hall near Hathersage, Fenny Bentley Hall, Tissington Hall, Eyam Hall and Hartington Hall, all of which are built in the solid, Peakland vernacular style from the easily-worked gritstone, with stone-mullioned windows and gritstone-slate roofs. North Lees Hall, a battlemented three-storey tower house dated to the sixteenth century, was a home of the well-known Peakland family of the Eyres, which came to England with the Conqueror. Robert Eyre, of Highlow Hall, is said to have installed his seven sons in properties within sight of each other – and himself – at Offerton, Upper and Nether Shatton, Crookhill, North Lees, Moorseats and Hazelford, all of which have halls of the right antiquity to make this attractive tale a possibility. An even earlier, fourteenth century Eyre house existed at Padley, near Grindleford, of which only part of the gatehouse remains, now used as a chapel in remembrance of two Roman Catholic martyrs who died for their faith in the Armada year of 1588.

Many of these great landowning families were responsible for the first enclosures of the common fields which began in the late Middle Ages, and was finally concluded by the various Acts of Parliamentary Enclosure in the eighteenth and nineteenth centuries. It was these formal and highly detailed pieces of legislation, which could take years to enact and cost thousands of pounds, which gave the Peak its distinctive geometrical network of drystone walls, such an important feature of the landscape today. As early as 1697, Celia Fiennes noted on her journey through Derbyshire 'you see neither hedge nor tree but only low drye stone

Hartington Hall, built in 1611 by the Bateman family, is an excellent example of seventeenth-century vernacular architecture. It enjoys a new life as one of the most imposing Youth Hostels in the Peak.

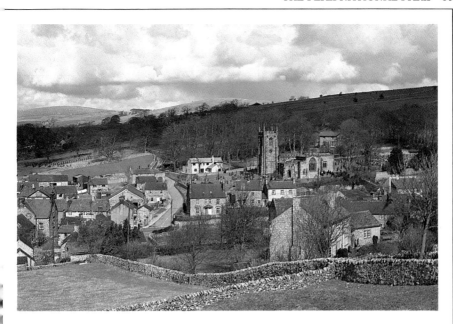

Hartington was granted the first recorded market charter in the Peak when King John gave the right to hold a Wednesday market to William de Ferrers, Earl of Derby, in 1203. The parish church of St Giles dominates this view of the village.

walls round some ground'. Many of the drystone walls seen today were built during this period, representing monumental efforts of labour over many years and standing as a tribute to the craftsmen of two centuries ago.

The other great plank of the medieval and post-medieval economy of the Peak District was lead mining. It is known that lead has been obtained from the White Peak at least since Roman times, and it is certain that it must have been in great demand for roofing and other building purposes for the castles, great houses, monasteries and religious houses erected in the great period of medieval building. In the Pipe Rolls of 1170, reference is made to lead from Derbyshire being sent to Westminster and Woodstock for the King's building works. In 1195, the Tideslow Mines, near Tideswell produced 2,600 loads (about 650 tons) of ore, and such was the productivity of the Peak District mining fields, some ore may even have been exported, like the 200 tons which was sent to Clairvaux Abbey in France in the late twelfth century. The Domesday Book records lead smelting sites at Bakewell, Ashford, Matlock and Wirksworth, so the ancient laws which govern the administration and control of the White Peak ore fields could well go back to Saxon days.

The framework of these complex laws was laid down at an inquisition in 1288, but they were summarized in Edward Manlove's *Rhymed Chronicle*, first published in 1653. Manlove was Steward of Wirksworth Barmote Court, one of several which still meet, with a Barmaster and jury of twelve 'miners' to adjudicate disputes. Some indication of the severity of these laws can be judged from this verse from Manlove's poem:

'For Stealing Ore twice from the Miners,
The Thief that's taken, twice fined shall be,
But the third time he commits such theft,
Shall have a Knife stuck through his Hand to th'Haft.
Into the Stow, and there till Death shall stand,
Or loose himself by cutting loose his Hand.'

Lead was such a precious commodity, and so easily accessible in the Peak, that huge fortunes were made in the hey-day of the industry, which was probably from 1700 to 1750, when at least 10,000 miners were at work. Almost every field in the limestone pastures of the White Peak still bears evidence of lead mining activity, the disturbed hillocks of waste spar now covered in grass, and the abandoned shafts, of which there may be at least 50,000, covered in often unstable piles of stones. These are usually the remains of the miners' 'coes', huts where they would leave their working tools, and a change of clothes for when they descended the shaft, after perhaps spending half the day working on their smallholdings.

The larger veins of lead, which run across country for miles, were known as 'rakes', while smaller off-shoots were 'scrins'. Aerial photographs of the area still show these centuries-old workings scarring the limestone pastures in a tracery of pock-marked craters. The Derbyshire lead miners, as Professor Hoskins has said, left no stone unturned in their feverish search for the precious ore. The larger rakes, which can be 500 ft (152 m) deep or more, are often screened by spindly shelter belts of ash trees, which served the double purpose of keeping cattle away from grassed areas poisoned or 'bellanded' by lead, and from the deep and dangerous vertical rakes. Several of the ancient words used by the lead miners, who are known locally by the generic term of 't'owd man', have passed into our modern language. An example is 'nicking', which was the word used if one miner took over the claim of another who had failed to work the mine, for whatever reason.

The greatest single enemy of the Peakland lead

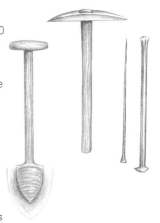

Lead miners' tools. The wooden bucket, used to lift ore up a shaft, was known as a 'kibble' and the rectangular metal dish was used as a measure for the ore.

Magpie Mine, near Sheldon, is the most complete lead mine remaining in the Peak. Note the round, Cornish chimney on the right and the metal winding gear of the last, unsuccessful mining attempt of the 'fifties in the centre.

miner was not another miner, nor the complex and archaic laws, but water. Below a certain level in a rake or scrin, the water table was reached, but such were the profits to be won from lead mining (one mine extracted £50,000 worth of lead in three years in the 1730s), it was worth the considerable expense of having the mine 'unwatered'. This was achieved by the construction of a tunnel or adit through the rock to drain the mine of its water. These tunnels, known as 'soughs', were usually driven from a lower level in an adjacent or deeper valley, which could often be two or three miles from the mine itself. More than thirty of these soughs existed by 1700, and they materially altered the water table of the White Peak. Many still carry large volumes of water which feed into the limestone rivers.

The most complete and interesting remains of a lead mine in the Peak are those preserved as a field centre by the Peak District Mines Historical Society at Magpie Mine, near Sheldon. This complex and fascinating collection of buildings, now empty and full of ghostly memories, represents a mine worked on and off for well over two hundred years, and shows most of the features of a typical Peakland lead mine. Its main sough, driven a mile underground to the River Wye at Ashford between 1873 and 1881, was one of the last major soughs to be constructed, but it failed to save the mine, despite the £18,000 cost of the exercise. Some years before, Magpie Mine was the scene of 'violence on the mine' over disputed rights by rival groups of miners to a vein of lead. There were sentries mounted on the surface and underground fighting until finally the inevitable happened in 1833, when three miners were suffocated by sulphurous fires deliberately ignited by their rivals. Magpie Mine, now scheduled as an ancient monument, represents Peak District lead mining in microcosm, from its older, square 'Derbyshire' pumping house chimney to the round 'Cornish' chimney and powder house, which date from 1839. The last, unsuccessful, attempt to drain the workings was made as recently as the 1950s, and the rusting, corrugated iron buildings from that enterprise are probably the oddest and youngest protected structures in the national park.

Lead mining left its mark on the landscape in other ways too, for the numerous 'Bole Hills' marked on the map show where the early miners constructed their primitive lead smelting hearths. These were usually on a westward-facing hilltop to catch the wind and force a draught for the fires which would partially melt the lead ore into the saleable ingots or 'pigs'. There are a large number of these bole sites on the eastern gritstone moors, overlooking the Derwent Valley, which face the full force of the prevailing winds, but later cupolas or enclosed furnaces were used and by 1811, at least twenty of these smoke-belching chimneys were recorded in the district.

Lead was not the only part of the mineral wealth of the Peak to be exploited during these years, when many now-peaceful dales echoed with the sounds of men at work, and were filled with the noise and smoke of industry.

The copper mines at Ecton Hill, above the winding River Manifold near Warslow, are estimated to have earned the Dukes of Devonshire a profit of £1,300,000 during the eighteenth century, and are said to have paid for many of the palatial developments at Chatsworth, and the building of The Crescent at Buxton. In 1786, when production was at its peak, about 4,000 tons of copper ore were brought to the surface by a workforce of about 300, and evidence of this enormous industry can still be seen in the vast waste tips which scar the surface of Ecton Hill today.

The powerful, rushing waters of the River Wye, seen here in Chee Dale, attracted the first industrialists like Richard Arkwright.

That abundant and troublesome supply of water which was such a problem to the old lead miners, (incidentally never such a problem at Ecton) became an attractive bonus to the next great entrepreneurs of the Industrial Revolution – the great eighteenth-century mill-owners. Water power was to be the first great impetus towards an industrialized Britain, and the fast-flowing rivers of the Peak were ideal to power the cotton mills of men like Richard Arkwright and Jedediah Strutt.

It was the greatest of the Peak rivers, the Derwent, which first attracted Arkwright, and in 1771 he became the first to apply water power to drive his textile factory at Cromford, just outside the national park. It is interesting to note that his second mill at Cromford, built in 1777, used water from an old lead mine sough to power its machinery. Within the next five years, Arkwright built further mills at Cressbrook and Bakewell, in the valley of the Wye.

Of course, water power had been used for centuries to power corn mills and later some lead-crushing mills, in the Peak. But Arkwright was the first to bring industrial methods and conditions to the Peak, and in the Old House Museum at Bakewell, lovingly restored by the Bakewell Historical Society, we can see how some of the 350 employees at his mill lived, for it housed six families of his workers. At Lumford a fine group of his workers' cottages still stands near the mill site and packhorse bridge,

Crag Mill, Wildboarclough, was originally a silk mill, and later the village post office.

although the mill is gone. Arkwright's Bakewell mill was a constant source of trouble to him because of a long-running dispute with the Duke of Rutland, who claimed it took water from his fishing and affected his own corn mills on the river.

The present Cressbrook Mill, a beautifully-proportioned and pedimented building of about 1815, complete with a little bell tower, is not Arkwright's although it stands on the site of his 1779 building. The state of the present Cressbrook Mill is giving the Park authority cause for concern, as it is at present mainly empty. A later owner of the Cressbrook Mill was William Newton, the so-called 'Minstrel of the Peak', an understanding master who took a personal interest in the welfare and conditions of his young apprentices. Quite the opposite, if you believe *The Memoirs of Robert Blincoe* published in 1832, of what was happening at Litton Mill, a couple of miles upstream. Blincoe was employed as an apprentice at Litton Mill from 1803 to 1814 under the cruel mastership of Ellis Needham, but nowadays his somewhat melodramatic memoirs are regarded as a 'ghosted' piece of propaganda in advance of the long overdue Factory Act of 1833.

Not all the Peak District mills were involved in cotton production, however, and on the western edge of the Park at Wildboarclough stand the imposing three-storey remains – later to be a post office – of the offices of Crag Mill, which produced silk and carpets for the Great Exhibition of 1851.

From medieval times, the main forms of transport for the products of Peak industry, from wool to cotton and from lead to copper, was packhorse or horse and cart. Many of the ancient packhorse routes, like the Portway across the limestone plateau, have been used at least since Roman times and probably from prehistory. The winding trains of packhorses, perhaps forty or fifty strong, could carry up to two hundredweights of lead per animal, and the routes they took still wind across the otherwise trackless moors to be followed today by ramblers from the nearby cities. Jagger's Clough, on the eastern side of Kinder Scout, perpetuates the name of the leaders of these packhorse trains, who were named after the German 'Jaeger' ponies they used. Where the way was difficult, either through bad weather or conditions under foot, wayside crosses were erected, like those at Edale Cross, at the top of Jacob's Ladder between Kinder and

The jingling bells of packhorse trains were once a common sound on Peakland trails. The 'Jaggers' who led them were the equivalent of today's juggernaut drivers.

Brown Knoll, and Hope Cross, on the Roman Road between Glossop and Navio. Typically narrow packhorse bridges, just wide enough for horses to pass in single file with low parapets to avoid the swinging panniers (baskets) on either side of the animals, are common in the Peak. There are examples at Bakewell, and the reconstructed ones from Derwent at Slippery Stones in the Upper Derwent valley, and in the Goyt Valley near Goytsclough Quarry. But perhaps the most famous of all is Viator's Bridge at Milldale on the River Dove, made famous by that character's remark in Izaak Walton's *The Compleat Angler*: 'Why! a mouse can hardly go over it; it is but two fingers broad.' These ancient routes were often adopted by

Left Viator's Bridge, Milldale.

the turnpike roads from the middle of the eighteenth century, such as Thomas Telford's famous Snake Pass route of 1821.

The railway age came surprisingly early to the seemingly difficult terrain of the Peak. Originally proposed as a canal (the stations were known as 'wharfs') the Cromford and High Peak Railway was designed to link the Cromford Canal and the Peak Forest Canal at Whaley Bridge across the 1,000 foot high White Peak limestone plateau. Engineer Josiah Jessop used a system of inclined planes and stationary steam engines to haul the wagons up the hills, with horses as the motive power along the level sections. The thirty-three mile line was opened in 1830, and steam locomotives took over three years later. It was mainly used for local traffic, particularly the transport of milk from local farms, before it closed in 1967.

The Buxton–Ashbourne line was opened at the end of the 'Railway Age' in 1894, but closed a few months after the Cromford and High Peak line in 1967. These two lines converge at the charmingly-named Parsley Hay station, and are now converted to walking and riding routes after purchase by the National Park authority. The Ashbourne–Buxton

Cyclists replace steam trains on the former Buxton–Ashbourne line, now known as the Tissington Trail.

The Monsal Dale viaduct over the River Wye was the target of John Ruskin's wrath when it was built in 1863. Now it forms part of the Monsal Trail, and is a protected structure.

route, purchased in 1968, is now known as the Tissington Trail, and the Cromford and High Peak route, bought in 1971, is now the High Peak Trail, and links with the southern part owned by Derbyshire County Council.

Perhaps the most ambitious rail route through the Peak was the London–Midland line, which was given permission to push through from Rowsley to Buxton in 1860. Neither the Duke of Devonshire nor the Duke of Rutland wished the line to go through the landscaped parklands of their estates, but eventually a compromise was reached when the line was 'undergrounded' through the Haddon estate, and special stations were constructed for the Duke of Rutland (at Bakewell) and the Duke of Devonshire (at Hassop).

The ten-mile stretch of line which threaded through the Wye valley was a great challenge for the railway engineers, involving long stretches of tunnel and soaring viaducts to take the line above the rushing waters of the river. John Ruskin made one of his most famous and most-quoted outbursts against the construction of the now-protected Monsal Dale viaduct when it opened in 1863. 'The valley is gone and the Gods with it, and now every fool in Buxton can be at Bakewell in half an hour and every fool in Bakewell at Buxton; which you think a lucrative process of exchange – you Fools everywhere.' The line closed in 1968, and was purchased by the National Park in 1980, to now become the Monsal Trail. There are long-standing plans by Peak Rail Operations to eventually re-open this spectacular line to steam trains.

Other major cross-Pennine routes were constructed via the infamous Woodhead Tunnel through Longdendale in 1847 (another line now closed and proposed as a 'leisure route'), and the 1894 Edale–Hope Valley route, now the only Manchester–Sheffield passenger route threading the Peak, via the Cowburn and Totley Tunnels.

It is interesting to reflect that some of the 'navvies' on these later railway routes may later have been involved in the last great civil engineering projects in the Peak, the construction of the huge reservoirs which were to flood the Upper Derwent, Goyt and Etherow Valleys. The Derwent dams of Howden, Derwent and Ladybower, are probably the most famous, and the self-contained community of 'Tin Town' at Birchinlee, is still remembered as the fifteen-year home for many of the navvies and their families while the Howden and Derwent Dams were being built in the early years of the twentieth century.

The deep, Dark Peak gritstone valleys were ideal for damming to provide drinking water for the surrounding cities, and today, the reservoirs are popular places for visitors and support a surprisingly varied wildlife.

The same can be said of those disused railway tracks which snake across the limestone plateau. Since their closure, many have become nature reserves, and the habitat for many rare species of wildlife and flowers not found elsewhere on the 'improved' agricultural pastures of the White Peak.

Nature has a way of fighting back, as we shall see in the next chapter on the natural history of the Peak.

The two original bores of the Woodhead Railway Tunnel in Longdendale (on the left) are now sealed and used to underground power transmission lines.

Walkers enjoy a peaceful stroll alongside the Ladybower Reservoir.

5 **At the crossroads**

It was one of those rare, scorchingly-hot midsummer days when the relentless rays of the sun reflected off the white walls of limestone with eye-blinking intensity. Not the day, we decided, to tramp across the open limestone plateau, where even the skylarks had abandoned their spiralling silver corkscrews of song to shelter from the blistering heat.

We opted for the cool greenness of the ash, beech and wych elm woods of Lathkill Dale, part of the Derbyshire Dales National Nature Reserve (NNR) and one of the gems of the national park's natural heritage. The Lathkill is a rarity among English rivers, for it runs through limestone for the whole of its length, from its source near Lathkill Head Cave to its confluence with the River Bradford at Alport.

The fact that the Lathkill is a pure limestone river and does not rise, like most of our upland rivers, on acidic soils, gives it an amazingly rich and diverse flora and fauna, and was one of the main reasons for the Nature Conservancy Council's NNR designation in 1972. It is also blessed with a concessionary

Reflections in the River Lathkill.

footpath threading its three-mile length, which gives a fascinating insight into one of the few largely natural landscapes of the Peak. The steep walls of the limestone crags were too precipitous to support grazing, so the hand of Man has had little effect on the plant and animal communities here, which include many national rarities.

Rarities are a recurring feature of the Peak's natural history for, as has already been stated, it stands at the crossroads between Highland and Lowland Britain. So whether you approach it from the north or west, south or east, you will find plants and animals at the very limits of their range in Britain. This makes it a Mecca for birdwatchers and botanists.

Examples of this 'borderland' peculiarity on the moors of the Dark Peak are cowberry, crowberry, bearberry and cloudberry, all of which reach their southern limits in the Pennines here. The delicate blue ivy-leaved bellflower, on the other hand, is at its eastern limit in the moorland springs and flushes, while the ring ouzel and mountain hare are other northern types at their southern limit on the Dark Peak moors.

Lathkill Dale is another place where you can find plants 'at their limits'. The warm, south-facing slopes mark the north-western limit of the stemless thistle, common on the downlands of the south, while bird cherry and mossy saxifrage, characteristic northern species, mark their southernmost boundaries on the damper, north-facing dale-sides.

Long before its official recognition by the Nature Conservancy Council, the charms of the Lathkill were well known to Charles Cotton, the 'Piscator' of the second part of *The Compleat Angler*. The Lathkin, as he spelt it, was 'by many degrees, the purest and most transparent stream that I ever saw, either at home or abroad.' And it bred, he said, 'the reddest and the best Trouts in England.'

As we set off from the clapper bridge at Lathkill Lodge, below Over Haddon, speckle-sided trout glided silently, heads into the current, through the crystal clear water. On the mine-riddled crags alongside the broad path (home of bats like the pipistrelle) lime-loving plants like the bright scarlet herb robert, the yellow stars of stonecrop, small scabious and salad burnet, turned the apparently barren rockfaces into colourful rock gardens which would be the envy of many a backyard enthusiast. Stands of great hairy willow-herb and the fragrant

The dipper is a common sight on fast-flowing limestone rivers.

Ash trees find a foothold on the scree slopes of Lathkill Dale.

froth of meadowsweet (once used to freshen the air in medieval houses when added to the rushes used for floor covering) lined the banks of the river. The red-veined, powder blue petals of meadow cranesbill, another member of the geranium family like herb robert, provided vivid splashes of colour. This common wayside flower is known locally as 'thunderclouds' because its blooms often presage July thunderstorms.

As we entered the welcoming shade of Palmerston Wood, the sunlight streamed through the woodland canopy, illuminating carpets of colour in the clearings. Red and white campion and tall yellow spikes of mullein caught the sun, while in the deeper shade, wood anemone, dog's mercury and ransoms (or wild garlic) covered the scree-littered slopes. Deeper in the trees, especially the inaccessible woodlands of Meadow Place and Low Wood on the opposite southern bank, the rare, purple-flowered spikes of mezereon had heralded spring some months before, and had now reverted to an inconspicuous shrub in the rich understorey of hazel, dogwood and guelder rose. These south-bank ash woods along the Lathkill are among the finest 'climax' ashwoods in Britain, second only to the famous Dovedale woodlands in the Peak, according to the Nature Conservancy Council. The woodlands on the north side of the dale, through which we were walking, are much more recent in origin, having been re-established after lead mining activities ceased just over a century ago. Wych elm and beech now cloak the remains of the Lathkill and Mandale Mines, but the massive ivy-clad structure of 'the Bob', or main retaining wall of the engine house of the Mandale Mine, is still visible among the trees. It was strange to think that this now peaceful valley was once a hive of industry, and filled by the sounds of men at work.

The path led us down to the river once more, and the hum of insects, including darting and hovering dragonflies, filled the heavy hair. Then suddenly, almost sensed rather than seen, the iridescent flash of a kingfisher zipped downstream. Red-beaked moorhens fussed their second brood of ugly, black-fluffy youngsters into the cover of the reeds as we passed, disturbing the mirror-calm of the river.

Where the smoothness of the flatter reaches was broken by gurgling rapids below the artificial weirs, (created to assist the spawning trout) white-spattered rocks announced the presence of perhaps the most typical bird of the dales. The white-bibbed dipper, bobbing and curtsying on its midstream perch like an overgrown wren, hunts by boldly entering the torrent and half walking and half swimming upstream in search of water beetles, insect larvae or crustaceans. Among its prey in the Lathkill or similar limestone rivers, might be that miniature lobster, the freshwater crayfish, locally known as a 'crawkie'. Crayfish will only tolerate the cleanest, clearest waters such as these. The sulphur-bellied grey wagtail is another common sight for birdwatchers in these limestone dales, although unfortunately we did not see one that day.

As we emerged from the trees at the upper end of Palmerston Wood, noting the clearance of the invasive and alien sycamore which had been undertaken by the Nature Conservancy Council, the bright glare of the sunshine showed we had entered a completely different world. We were now in the open grassland of the upper dale, where hawthorn scrub provided the only tree cover for 'charms' of flocking goldfinches, which twittered excitedly across the steeper slopes in their endless search for thistle seed heads. The close, sheep and rabbit-cropped grass supported creeping fragrant mats of purple-flowered thyme, sky-blue harebells and the red and yellow flowers of bird's foot trefoil (also known as 'bacon and eggs'). Up to fifty-four species

The freshwater crayfish, locally known as a 'crawkie'.

Limestone scars
and crags near the head
of Lathkill Dale.

The brown argus
butterfly, which feeds on
rockrose.

of plant have been recorded in a square metre of
this herb-rich grassland, in sharp contrast with the
paucity of the gritstone moors. Elsewhere, the rich,
butter yellow flowers of rockrose spread across the
thin, stony pastures, and my naturalist companion
observed that this lime-loving trailing perennial
was the food plant of the lovely brown argus
butterfly. Just on cue, the beautiful chocolate brown,
orange-spotted wings of a brown argus appeared,
to be joined by another in a dizzy, spiralling dance
in the shimmering air above the dale floor.

Lathkill Dale is the scene of an annual butterfly
monitoring exercise, conducted each summer when
a fixed route is walked through the dale and notes
are made of the different species and their numbers.
Among the more common species recorded here
are the meadow brown, small tortoiseshell, and
green-veined white, and the survey has shown the
dale to be one of the best sites in the country for the
orange tip.

High on the daleside one summer a few years
ago, I was lucky enough to spot the bright orange-
yellow of a clouded yellow butterfly, recorded that
season in the dale for the first time in thirty years.
Maybe, we reflected, a more restrained use of
herbicides by the farming community will lead to an
increase in butterfly numbers, just as the banning of
certain pesticides has seen an increase in birds of
prey in the dales.

By now, we were out in the more spectacular
scenery of the upper dale, where prominent white

scars of limestone are exposed high in the sweeping dalesides. A kestrel hung in the hot up-current of air above the crags, searching with razor-sharp eyes for the unwise movement which might mean death for a short-tailed vole or field mouse. A heron flapped lazily overhead before descending to resume its constant search for aquatic prey.

We passed the site of Carter's Mill, a former corn-grinding mill, where the river cascades prettily over a dam formed of the rare rock formation known as tufa. This rock is only found in pure limestone streams and rivers like the Lathkill, when calcium carbonate is deposited on mosses and rocks in much the same way as stalactites and stalagmites are deposited in underground caves. So pure is the Lathkill that it is one of the places where tufa is still being formed, in the mill pool beyond Carter's Mill.

We passed the entrance to Cales Dale on our left and the remains of the ancient sheepwash, built by the monks of nearby One Ash Grange in the twelfth or thirteenth century. The overhanging wall of the resurgence cave of Lathkill Head, where the river can emerge in a spectacular torrent in times of winter flood, looked cool and inviting. Now the dale narrowed and deepened between towering walls of limestone, and in the damp bottom of the dale, we were treated to a flamboyant display of another of the Lathkill's great rarities. The luxuriant stands of the beautiful deep blue flowers of Jacob's ladder in the dale are among the largest anywhere in the country, and the prominent golden-yellow stamens looked dusty with pollen as we passed.

Eventually we climbed out through the boulder choke by Ricklow Quarry at the end of the dale and out on to the open plateau, where a white-rumped wheatear scolded us from a tumbled-down drystone wall as we approached the Monyash road.

The delicate blue stars of Jacob's ladder, a rare flower which is the sole British member of the Polemoniaceae family.

It had been one of those magical days to treasure in your memory, but although Lathkill Dale perhaps represents the cream of the Peak's natural history heritage, and we had been exceptionally lucky to see so much that day, most of the species we saw can be found in any of the limestone dales, such as the Dove, Manifold or Bradford. These are the highlights for the naturalist, with an unrivalled range of largely unspoilt and unpolluted habitats, typified by that walk through Lathkill Dale.

The limestone plateau is sparse by comparison, mainly through its continuous exploitation by Man as a farmer over 4,000 or more years. After the large-

Early purple orchids, indicators of undisturbed pastures.

scale clearance of the wildwood, which probably began in the Mesolithic period and went on into medieval times, the traditional farming regime on the high limestone plateau has been mainly pastoral, although large areas were still heathland until the Enclosure Movement of the seventeenth and eighteenth centuries.

The light, loamy soil supported permanent pastures for the grazing herds of cattle and sheep, except for some arable use around villages, where lynchets and ridge-and-furrow still show the evidence of former cultivation. Today, the majority of those traditional meadows, cut once or twice a year for hay to see the stock through the long, hard winters, are gone and replaced by the monotonous monoculture of rye-grass leys, or short-term pastures cut for silage and regularly ploughed and re-seeded.

Occasionally, however, you can come across 'unimproved' fields full of flowers like ox-eye daisies, meadow saxifrage, marjoram, cowslip and early purple orchids, which are in sharp contrast to the uniform bright green of the short-term leys of the 'improved' pastures. Local farmers have been encouraged to retain these increasingly rare herb-rich hay meadows through the National Park authority's Integrated Rural Development experiment in Monyash and Longnor, and some were actually paid on the number of wild flower species in their fields.

Above these fields, and nesting in them, tumbling flocks of lapwings, or peewits, can fill the sky and more rarely, the long down-curved bill of the curlew is seen, and the spine-tingling, bubbling song of this elegant wader sounds across the bleak, open plateau. Skylarks trill in the summer skies, and in winter, large flocks of fieldfares and redwings, migrants from Arctic Scandinavia and even Siberia, cast across the fields in search of insects.

Interesting 'mini-habitats' have been created in the disused railway cuttings and embankments now followed by the Tissington, High Peak, Monsal and Manifold walking and riding 'leisure routes'. Here, bloody cranesbill, kidney vetch and the nationally rare Nottingham catchfly thrive where steam trains once passed. Particularly attracted to these man-made habitats, but rarely seen because of their nocturnal habits, are animals like the fox and badger, while white-bibbed weasels can sometimes be seen dashing across the roads between the drystone walls, where they make their homes, and

Weasels nest in the cavities of drystone walls.

Winter frost and snow grip the soft peat hags of Kinder Scout in their icy hold.

occasionally pop up inquisitively on hind legs to stare at intruders.

As early as 1688, that pioneer of British botany, John Ray, noted a Peak District oddity which again illustrates Nature's amazing adaptability and tolerance of Man's activities. He recorded the pincushions of spring sandwort as one of the few plants 'on the barren earth they dig out of the shafts of lead mines'. The delicate white stars of spring sandwort, known locally as leadwort from its preferred habitat, are still a common sight on the many abandoned spoil heaps near old lead mines and rakes. This astonishing little plant is very rare elsewhere, and can withstand concentrations of normally highly toxic lead and zinc which would kill most other plants. Alpine penny-cress, yellow mountain pansy, eyebright and autumn gentians are other plants of the lead rakes, and on a spoil tip

Lead-tolerant spring sandwort covers old lead-mine spoil heaps in dazzling white pin-cushions.

along the High Peak Trail, no fewer than thirty-five different species of flowering plants and grasses, including four species of orchid, have been recorded in a square metre of this apparently sterile habitat.

Nowhere in the Peak is apparently more barren, at first glance, than the high peat moors of the Dark Peak. The highest points of the park, such as Kinder Scout, Bleaklow and Black Hill, could also be described as the most depressing, at least from the botanical point of view. The walker John Hillaby aptly described these northern moors in his *Journey through Britain*:

> 'From the botanical point of view, they are examples of land at the end of its tether. All the life has been drained off or burnt out, leaving behind only the acid peat. You can find nothing like them anywhere else in Europe.'

The bleak, chocolate-brown dunes of sticky peat stretch for mile after mile like a murky ocean frozen in time. They are split by steep-sided 'groughs' which partly drain the sodden landscape, and the upstanding 'hags' or banks of peat which can steam, like manure, in the sun. Hillaby thought that manure was the best analogy for Kinder Scout, which looked to him as if it was 'entirely covered in the droppings of dinosaurs'. The bare, heavily-dissected peat depressed him. 'The faint cheep of (meadow) pipits sounds like the last ticks of a clock that has almost run down', he complained.

As Hillaby explained, these great wildernesses of the Peak, so precious and close to the 'bogtrotters' of Sheffield and Manchester, are examples of the end product of a gradual degradation of plant life. After the glaciers of the Ice Age retreated, this land was covered in deciduous forest, the remains of which are still sometimes exposed in the sides of groughs, when the bleached boles of those prehistoric trees are revealed again. But as the climate deteriorated, and Man the farmer set to work clearing, burning and grazing the former forests, that once luxuriant tree cover disappeared. Bright green sphagnum moss started to form in the ill-drained patches, and the land became progressively more sour and acid. In the end, only acid-resistant plants like heather, bilberry, cotton grass and the evergreen crowberry could survive, and today, on about sixteen square miles of the more heavily-eroded parts of Black Hill, Bleaklow and Kinder, even these have gone. The peat,

Cotton grass colonizes poorly drained peat bogs with its fluffy white fruiting heads. It may have given the name to the many 'featherbed mosses' of the southern Pennines.

Autumn burnishes the leaves of this beech in the Upper Derwent Valley, contrasting strongly with the gloom of the coniferous forest across the reservoir.

remains of those former plant communities which bacteria could not break down, is gradually being washed or blown away, and eventually, these bleak plateaux will be worn down to their gritstone bedroc But a moorland erosion project, partly sponsored by the National Park authority, has shown that fenced-off areas protected from grazing sheep soon recover and can be re-colonized by heather and bilberry. Grazing pressure and atmospheric pollution – or 'acid rain' – have proved to be among the main causes of modern moorland erosion.

But although Kinder Scout remains 'the most featureless, disconsolate, bog-quaking, ink-oozing moor you ever saw' as John Derry so accurately described it in the classic walker's guide, *Across the Derbyshire Moors*, there is still a great deal of wildlife interest in these forbidding places. Perhaps the best way to show just what riches there are in the Dark Peak moorlands is to describe another walk I took one spring along the length of Derwent Edge in the north-east of the national park.

We started from the strangely alien landscape of the Derwent Valley reservoirs, which always remind me more of the coniferous forests and lakes of north-west Canada than the Peak District. The largest expanses of open water in the park are to be found here, in the triple reservoirs of Howden, Derwent and Ladybower, which provide water for the industrial cities of Sheffield, Derby, Nottingham and Leicester. The steep-sided reservoirs and acid waters are not attractive to many water birds or waders, which need shallows and muddy spits to encourage their main sources of food, but just occasionally, the ardent 'twitcher' may glimpse a rare passage migrant, such as the ospreys regularly recorded over the Goyt Valley reservoirs of Errwood and Fernilee. We were lucky on this day too, for as we walked along the forestry track along the side of the Derwent Reservoir, below us in the water were a pair of red-breasted mergansers. Their vivid scarlet eyes and spiky 'punk' crests identified them instantly, and their viciously-hooked sawbills were obviously being employed in an underwater search for the rainbow trout, which the water authority provides primarily for human anglers!

The thickly-regimented stands of spruce and larch cast a coniferous gloom over this part of the walk, with only the glossy green of the equally-alien rhododendrons brightening the scene. But even these dark and apparently sterile coniferous plantations, which cloak both sides of the Upper Derwent valley, are not the wildlife deserts they are sometimes thought to be. Here in the Upper Derwent (whose name, you may recall, originally meant the river abounding in oaks), some of our rarest birds of prey find their secluded homes, and the area includes the British stronghold of that elegant and rare raptor, the goshawk. Goldcrests, siskins in winter, and occasional summer 'irruptions' of crossbills also add interest to these man-made forests, where the rarer, native red squirrels also find their last Peak District habitat.

Of course, the native oak woodlands which originally clothed the sides of the Derwent, and most of the rest of the Dark Peak after the retreat of the glaciers, are much richer in wildlife than commercial coniferous plantations of the Upper Derwent, Alport Dale, and the Woodlands Valley. But pockets of that original tree cover are still to be found, especially in the less-accessible Dark Peak cloughs, where gritstone boulders make it difficult for nibbling sheep to hamper the process of natural regeneration.

These 'relict' oak and birch woodlands, such as Ladybower Wood, a Derbyshire Wildlife Trust reserve behind the Ladybower Inn just east of the southern end of the reservoir, are havens for the sort of wildlife which must have once been

Sessile oak, with leaf.

widespread in the Dark Peak. The oaks in these
scattered woods are of the upland, 'sessile' type,
recognizable by the fact that their acorns have no
stalks, and ground cover in these woods is
dominated by bilberry, whose luscious black fruits
are eagerly sought in late summer, and the
beautifully named wavy hair-grass. Ferns like the
broad buckler and hard fern enjoy the acid
conditions found in these woodlands, and flowers
typically include the tall, nodding purple heads of
foxglove. Ferocious wood ants also build their
massive nests among the leaf litter on the woodland
floor.

As oak trees support nearly 300 different species
of insects (compared with thirty-seven for spruce
and seventeen for larch), oak woods are obviously
very attractive to birds. Padley Gorge, a delightfully
wooded valley on the National Trust's Longshaw
estate near Grindleford, has become the regional
stronghold for the diminutive pied flycatcher, which
regularly makes the marathon journey from its
wintering quarters in the savanna belt of tropical
Africa to breed in specially provided nest boxes.
Other summer visitors to these lovely old
woodlands include the gaudy redstart, and the shy
wood warbler, more likely to be heard rather than
seen. Resident birds include the greater spotted
and green woodpeckers and those tree-trunk
gymnasts, the treecreeper and nuthatch. By the
bubbling streams coming off the moors, those
denizens of rushing water, the dipper and grey
wagtail, may be seen bobbing and curtsying.

On the woodland edges, both coniferous and
deciduous, two other great Peakland ornithological
rarities are found, in locations which are best kept
secret because of sadly declining numbers mainly
brought about through the destruction of their
preferred habitats. They are that mysterious
nocturnal master of camouflage, the moth-catching
nightjar, whose 'churring' song can be heard in
certain sites on the east of the park, and the black
grouse, or 'blackcock', which is now confined to a
single area in the Staffordshire moorlands. The
blackcock's elaborate courtship display, conducted
in special areas known as 'leks' is one of the sights in
the birdwatching world, and attracts large numbers
of 'twitchers' to these traditional arenas every
spring. But as long ago as 1789, an observer
reported: 'formerly these birds appeared in great
numbers in the Peak but now are very seldom seen'.

Much more common, and a constant companion

Grey wagtail, a denizen of
rocky cloughs.

Red grouse—king of the heather moors.

on our moorland walk along Derwent Edge, is the red grouse, the nearest thing we have to an exclusively British bird. No other creature has had a more profound effect on a British landscape than this plump, red-wattled game bird. Vast areas of heather moorland in the Dark Peak, to the north, and to a lesser extent, to the east and west of the national park are managed for sheep and for the benefit of the red grouse, and the income from shooting rights often exceeds that from the sheep which share their domain. How much poorer our Dark Peak moorlands would be, however, if it was not for this furry-footed resident of the high places. For the main food plant of the red grouse, essential also to its successful breeding and roosting, is heather.

Detailed and careful management regimes, including regular springtime burning of some areas of heather, not only create the familiar patchwork patterns of the moors, but also give the grouse exactly the sort of habitat it requires. The older, more woody heather gives the grouse the cover it needs to nest and roost in, while younger, nutritious shoots, encouraged after burning or 'swaling', are a major food source, along with insects like crane flies. Peak District moors have given the shooting fraternity some spectacular 'bags' over the years. The record is the 1,421½ brace (2,843 birds) which were shot by nine guns in a day on Broomhead Moor in 1913. 'The Glorious Twelfth' of August is the sign for certain of the access moors of the park to be closed on a rota basis so that walkers do not get in the way of the shooters. Shooting dates are published in the Park's information centres.

The gutteral chuckle of the red grouse, warning us to 'Go back, go back, back, back', had become a regular sound as we emerged by the ancient Cut Gate packhorse track on the open moor, on 1,791 ft (544 m) Margery Hill. Several grouse clattered into the sky to glide back to earth on down-curved wings as we passed, and later, as we crossed Howden Edge, one of our party nearly stepped on a covey of newly-hatched chicks, beautifully camouflaged against the rank moor grass.

Apart from the constant calls of the grouse, the ubiquitous meadow pipit is probably the most commonly seen bird of the high moors, although you may also see and hear birds like the curlew, dunlin and twite. The real gem for the moorland birdwatcher is, however, the beautiful, spangle-backed golden plover, the so-called 'watchman of the moors'. Its plaintive 'pee-eep' piping call is

Walkers on Ashop Moor, Kinder Scout, look across to the Alport Valley. Alport Castles are in the distance, on the extreme right.

passed from bird to bird across the moor to warn of approaching danger, and to our delight, we found we were able to imitate it easily, attracting answering calls from other golden plovers.

As we crossed a rocky clough, we had a superb grandstand view of one of these lovely birds, its black chest edged in white and its gold, black and white back feathers blending perfectly with the background. Lower down the clough, we thought we heard the 'chinking' call of the ring ouzel or mountain blackbird, a handsome bird with a distinctive white crescent gorget across its dusky-brown chest, which nests in these remote, rocky valleys.

Later, as we ascended to the high point of desolate Back Tor where John Derry thought the spirit of the moors had his throne, we had a distant view of a quartering hawk. It could have been a rare merlin, a goshawk or even a hen harrier, all of which have been recorded on these bleak moors.

Mountain hare—a
re-introduced species.

Cloudberry and
fruit—at its southern limit.

On the subject of birds of prey, it is interesting to note that the earliest written description of a golden eagle's nest in Britain was on Alport Castles in the Peak in 1668. Perhaps one day they will return, as they have in the Lake District, to soar again on huge wings above these desolate places. Certainly, the tide seems to be turning for these attractive hunters at the top of the moorland food chain, for that elegant master of the air, the peregrine falcon, has once again nested successfully in secret sites in the Peak after an absence of more than thirty years. It is an indictment of our society that these nest sites must be kept secret, and indeed placed under a twenty-four hour guard, when the birds are nesting Although 'protected' by law, their eggs are in great demand by unscrupulous collectors, fetching high prices on the black market. But how heartening it is to know that these superb hunters are back in the Peak.

Our eventful walk along the grand promenade of Derwent Edge was completed by the fleeting glimpse of a mountain hare, still embarrassingly carrying its white winter camouflage, which was unfortunately having the opposite effect against the sepia-brown moor grass. The story of these south Pennine mountain, or blue, hares is another one of a successful comeback – this time engineered by man.

They were part of the native fauna when the Ice Age glaciers departed, but their range gradually retracted due to habitat and climatic changes, until eventually they were only left in the sub-Arctic mountain stronghold of the Scottish Highlands. But during the nineteenth century, sportsmen re-introduced numbers of these small, rabbit-sized animals on to the moors of the Peak, and they seem to have thrived – although their seasonal change of coat still sometimes catches them out!

Mountain hares feed mainly on the tough leaves of heather in the winter, and young heather, fluffy, white-headed cotton grass and mat grass in summer. This is the typical vegetation of the high moors, with bilberry and cowberry growing abundantly on the lower slopes. On the even more exposed high tops Arctic plants like the aptly-named cloudberry, rarely found below 2,000 feet (and usually, therefore, in the clouds), are found. The cloudberry, with its delicate white flower and blackberry-like fruit, is quite common on Bleaklow and parts of Kinder, but is not found further south in England.

'Land at the end of its tether'—a peat bog on Black Hill.

Kinder's famous peat bogs, and the wetter 'flushes' below the edges, are the home for the remaining patches of bright-green sphagnum moss, which also seems to have been adversely affected by atmospheric pollution. Here and there, in these damp and boggy spots, you may also come across the attractive sticky red leaves of the insect-eating sundew, which has turned carnivorous in order to replace minerals missing from the acidic soil, the yellow flowers of bog asphodel and pale blue ivy-leaved bellflower, on the edge of its western range in Britain.

The call of the moors is strong, but nothing feels it more strongly than the spectacular male emperor moth, which can pick up the scent of a virgin female resting on the heather two miles away! Emperor moths, with four large eye spots on their wings to deter predators, depend on heather as one of their main food plants when in the caterpillar stage, and they are one of the most distinctive insects of the moors, along with the chattering, common green grasshopper.

Dark or White, the natural history of the Peak has something of interest for everyone, for as John Ruskin observed: 'In its very minuteness it is the most educational of all the districts of beautiful landscape known to me ... Derbyshire is a lovely child's alphabet; an alluring first lesson in all that is admirable ...'

But it is a landscape which needs protecting and sensitive management, as we will see in the next chapter of our story.

6 'A splendid achievement'

On 10th July, 1978, the House of Commons debated the Government's reaction to the Peak National Park's Structure Plan. It was a unique occasion, for the Peak was the only national park to produce a structure plan which laid down the broad land-use planning policies for its area. The Lake District, the other autonomous national park planning board, had a joint structure plan with Cumbria.

After outlining the Government's amendments to the park's proposed 'general presumption against mineral working', the Minister of State for the Environment, Mr Denis Howell, added:

> 'I conclude by saying that we recognize that the Peak Park is a splendid achievement, that the work carried out by the Board in managing the different activities taking place in the park is continually worthy of praise and is a great national asset both to the residents of the park and the many millions of people who visit the area each year.'

High praise indeed, but then this first national park has always been highly regarded in terms of its organization, its management activity, innovation, and the level of funding devoted to tackling the extraordinary pressures on its protected landscape.

Of all our ten British national parks, the Peak's administration and constitution most closely follows the structure recommended by Dower and Hobhouse in their seminal post-war reports. It is run by an independent and autonomous joint planning board, consisting of representatives of local county and district councils, and members nominated by the Minister, at the ratio of two to one. The staff of about 140, including planners, architects, information officers, land agents, surveyors, foresters and rangers, works solely on the Board's approved policies for the wise management of the park. Only the Lake District National Park, the second to be designated just three weeks after the Peak in May 1951, has a similar joint board – the other eight are administered by committees of the county councils within which they fall.

The Peak Board's structure, independence and the enormous pressures on its area, has enabled it to argue for and attract more resources than the other parks. Even so, its total budget for 1986/87 was only £2.6 million which represents, even if it was all spent on visitors, an annual bill of only 13p per head.

Currently, seventy-two per cent of the Park's finance comes from central government, in the form of a National Park Supplementary Grant, bid for annually and now argued for on the basis of need shown in five-year 'functional strategies', which each of the parks have to produce. The remaining twenty-eight per cent of Board finance is raised by precept from the six constituent counties within which the national park falls, the largest contributor, in area and level of support, being Derbyshire.

The National Park authority, like all other British national parks, has two primary statutory duties. These are:

- the protection and enhancement of its natural beauty, and
- the encouragement of public access to, and enjoyment of, the park.

Despite the commonly-held belief, the vast majority of land in the park is in private hands, and the Peak National Park, as the local planning authority, owns only four per cent itself. Fifteen per cent of the area is owned by water authorities, over ten per cent by the National Trust (the independent charity with which the national park is often confused), and the rest mainly by farmers and private landowners. National parks in England and Wales are not nationalized nor are they primarily wildlife reserves. They are living and working landscapes, so that in recent years, a third major purpose has been added to the long-standing twin roles in conservation and recreation. This is concern for the social and economic well-being of those who live and work in the park. Promotion of the 'local interest' has become as important a consideration to the National Park authority as its national responsibilities as custodian of a fine and often threatened landscape and the promotion of recreational opportunities.

About 40,000 people live in the Peak National Park, of which about 8,000 have jobs inside the area. A similar number of residents travel out to work in the surrounding towns and cities. There are estimated to be about 12,000 jobs within the national

Farming in the Dark Peak is a constant battle against the elements. This is near Lee House Farm, Upper Booth, Edale, with Brown Knoll under snow across the infant River Noe.

park, and a recent breakdown of the employment structure carried out by the Park authority revealed some significant trends.

Only ten per cent of the working population is now employed in agriculture, and only eighteen per cent in mining and quarrying. This compares with nineteen per cent in manufacturing industry and a growing fifteen per cent in tourism. Other service industries, such as energy, construction, transport and similar occupations, account for the vast majority of jobs within the park.

The trend away from the traditional farming and mining dual economy of the Peak since the war has been brought about by increasing mechanization, falling demand for minerals and the rationalization of many farming enterprises.

Although the Park authority has no direct powers

of industrial promotion or development, it has been active in preparing plans which have created many new jobs in manufacturing industry.

In recent years, for example, it has helped create 125 new jobs in advance factory developments at Bakewell, Tideswell, Longnor and Warslow, and further developments of this kind are planned for Bakewell, Youlgreave, Parwich and elsewhere under the Development Commission's Rural Development Programmes.

The primary aim of many of the authority's policies is to maintain living village communities with a balanced age and social structure, and to this end it has pressed for the retention of village schools, and housing to meet *local* needs. Conservation areas, with grants to help repairs, have been set up in a number of key villages throughout the park and help improve the living environment for local people and visitors alike.

Public transport services, which benefit both local people and visitors, have also been encouraged through subsidies to schemes like the Peak Wayfarer and Peak Pathfinder buses.

From the very start, the Peak National Park authority sought innovative and pioneering solutions to the many varying pressures and problems with which it was faced. Looking back, however, it is interesting to note that the Board's first annual report, published in 1953, refers to the main mineral problem confronting it as 'the determination of the outstanding limestone applications and the formulation of a policy for dealing with future applications'. The 1984/85 annual report still referred to minerals appeals as 'the greatest test of the Board's policies', and described how two major public inquiries into proposed extensions of the limestone quarries at Topley Pike and Eldon Hill had placed a considerable strain on the Board's modest resources.

Prominent and intrusive limestone quarries like Eldon Hill, dubbed 'the best known eyesore in the Peak' and on one of the highest points of the White Peak plateau near Castleton, obviously remain one of the greatest and most obvious threats to the park's landscape. The absence of any firm national policy on mineral extraction is a constant handicap to the National Park authority, together with the fact that most of this chemically-pure limestone currently goes for road and construction aggregate – surely a wasted resource. Some sites like Eldon

Grange Mill quarry, just outside the national park boundary near Aldwark, is however typical of the many limestone quarries which disfigure the White Peak.

The Hope Valley Cement Works, an eyesore for over eighty years, but an important local source of employment.

Hill, and the prominent Hope Valley Cement Works, were also in existence long before the national park was designated. Indeed, the chimney in the Hope Valley (not the same one incidentally) was MJBBaddeley's 'pet nightmare' in the 1903 edition of his *Thorough Guide to The Peak District*. And the Peak Board has always to consider that such disfigurements to the landscape are also a very important local source of employment, and could be seen as an extension, albeit on a massive scale, to the traditional mining employment of the area.

Another major extractive industry stems directly from those old lead workings. Fluorspar, used in the chemical and steel industries, utilizes the waste fluorite discarded by 't'owd man' as worthless 'gangue'. Nearly three quarters of Britain's home-produced fluorspar comes from the White Peak area, but waste disposal, usually in huge land-consuming tailings reservoirs, is a major problem. The Park recently approved a major new underground mine for fluorspar at Great Hucklow, which incorporated some subterranean back-filling of waste and safeguarded about 250 local jobs.

Other threats to the park are less obvious to the casual visitor, such as the widespread 'improvements' made by farming and forestry.

When John Dower wrote his report, it was thought that the continuation of traditional farming was a key requirement in national parks, and that efficient agriculture was compatible with national park purposes. Farming operations remained outside planning control. But that was before the days of 'agri-business' and the wholescale changes of the post war agricultural revolution which have been wrought over much of Britain as a result of pursuing high production objectives, encouraged by grants and other incentives. Even in the uplands this has led to intensification of production, farm amalgamation and loss of labour.

Rounding up sheep on the national park's Eastern Moors estate.

One of the most encouraging recent alternatives to this trend was pioneered by the Peak's Integrated Rural Development (IRD) experiment, where agricultural and other grants have been used for conservation and social ends. It has important lessons for other upland communities faced with changing agricultural policies.

The villages of Monyash, on the limestone plateau at the head of Lathkill Dale, and Longnor, on the gritstone ridge between the Dove and Manifold, were chosen as the project areas for this unique experiment in 1981.

Drystone walls and shelter belts grant-aided by the IRD scheme near Monyash.

The principle of IRD is to try to co-ordinate the schemes of the various grant-aiding agencies operating in the countryside for the overall benefit of the communities as a whole. Individually, these agencies can often compete against each other, resulting in conflict and confusion.

With most of the ideas coming from the villagers themselves, and with the National Park authority acting as co-ordinator, the experiment showed that the IRD principle was a practical possibility. A fifty per cent initial grant from the European Commission got the project off the ground, and later the Countryside Commission and English Tourist Board underwrote the continuing experiment.

Among the headline-grabbing 'alternative grant' systems which were adopted in Monyash and Longnor was one which paid farmers on the number of wild flowers in their hay meadows, and replaced the Ministry of Agriculture's spraying and improvement grants. Farmers were also paid on the maintenance and upkeep of their drystone walls, which created a new demand for the dying craft of walling in the two villages.

Such schemes had multiple benefits to the community, and on the landscape. Stone walls, for

Longnor village, showing the parish church and market hall (right), now a ceramic studio set up with IRD funding.

example, are a vitally important element in the Peakland landscape; they provide stock-proof enclosures for farmers, and their maintenance provides work for local, traditional craftsmen. Other schemes benefitted the local community more directly, for example a new village hall and children's play area at Monyash, and a new museum

and the revival of well-dressing in Longnor. Six new small businesses were set up, and ten new full-time jobs were created. Village life was revived and a new spirit of optimism initiated.

The Peak Board has also worked closely with the farming community since 1980 when farmers were required by the Ministry of Agriculture to consult the Board on operations for which they sought grants. This has opened the door to discussions on conservation and a new understanding of mutual problems is emerging. The same applies to co-operation with the Forestry Commission and water authorities, both of which have working arrangements with the Board and are increasingly building conservation and recreation elements into their policies and plans. In the past, much damage was done to open hillsides and hidden, fertile valleys by blanket planting of alien conifers and flooding by huge reservoirs. Ironically now, in places like the Goyt and the Upper Derwent Valleys, these public authorities work closely with the National Park on traffic management and recreation schemes for the benefit of the thousands of visitors who enjoy these new, man-made landscapes.

Among the early innovative solutions to the problem of providing access for the traditional visitors from the surrounding cities were the access

The ranger seen here at work in the Upper Derwent Valley is jointly funded by the National Park and the Severn Trent Water Authority.

Visitor pressure and footpath erosion on Mam Tor, where footpath restoration work has had to be carried out.

Volunteers at work repairing the footpath on Jacob's Ladder, Kinder Scout.

agreements, which the Peak, almost alone among national parks, has vigorously pursued to open up seventy-six square miles of moorland. The creation of the Tissington and High Peak Trails, from the derelict scars left by abandoned railway lines across the limestone plateau, has provided access for other types of recreational users, and the 'Routes for People' scheme segregated recreational from industrial traffic and provided car parks, picnic sites and waymarked walks for visitors in the White Peak area.

The pressure caused by those twenty million annual visits, together with the unique recreational and other amenities of the Peak National Park, recently prompted one outdoor writer to describe it as the most important national park in Western Europe. It is a weighty responsibility which the Park authority has always exercised with skill and ingenuity, despite limited resources.

A key role in easing the potential friction between visitor and local resident is played by the Peak's well-respected Ranger Service, originally provided to patrol just the moorland access areas, but which now covers the whole of the park with its distinctive Land Rovers. Scores of part-time volunteers back up the Ranger Service, and perform useful conservation tasks throughout the park, especially on the 5,000 miles of public footpaths in the area.

Above Interpretive display, Edale Information Centre.

Left A school group from Losehill Hall on a farm visit in the Hope Valley.

Just as important is the role undertaken by the Park's Information Service. Through eight centres around the park, the vital messages of conservation, recreation and the local interest are expounded and the landscape is explained, aided by an extensive range of publications, guided walks and talks.

Another 'first' for the Peak was the creation of the first National Park residential study centre in Britain at Losehill Hall, Castleton, which was opened by Princess Anne in 1972. It provides opportunities for people to learn about the character of the national park and the issues it faces. This 60-bed centre has also pioneered training in countryside-related skills, and gained an international reputation with its annual European conferences. The 'European connection' has been furthered by the Park's membership of the European Federation of Nature and National Parks, and in 1966, it was awarded the Diploma for nature conservation by the Council of Europe – the first in Britain.

This prestigious award has since been renewed four times but on each occasion, the inspecting working party has warned that if the industrial threats facing the park were not successfully countered, the diploma could not be awarded.

The positive side of the Park's work is probably best expressed in the National Park Plan, which all

Doxey Pool, on the National Park's Roaches estate on the Staffordshire Moors, has a legend of a mermaid, just like that of the Mermaid's Pool below Kinder Scout.

parks are required to produce to lay down their detailed policies on conservation and recreation. The Peak had been divided into 'natural' and 'rural' zones by the structure plan, and the National Park Plan further sub-divided the park into five 'recreational zones', which indicated the levels and types of recreational use thought appropriate. A high level of agreement was reached on the plan after an extensive consultation process.

Although most of the Board's work in conservation and recreation provision is achieved through persuasion and agreement on land owned by others, recently the Peak Park Board has taken advantage of opportunities to acquire land. Major acquisitions include the 6,400 acre Eastern Moors estate in 1984, the 1,000 acre Roaches estate in 1979, and the 4,500 acre Warslow Moors estate in 1986. It can now lead by example in showing how commercial farming management can go hand-in-hand with conservation and recreation objectives. The provision by the Board of camping and caravanning sites, hostels, 'camping barns' and cycle hire centres shows the Board's commitment to serving the recreational need of visitors. A positive approach to the encouragement of appropriate tourism, with the emphasis on staying visitors, is now an integral part of Board policy.

The Park's continuing responsibility was foreseen forty years ago in the Hobhouse Report, which concluded: 'The formidable list of problems which have forced themselves upon our attention indicate that the management of the Peak District National Park will call for balanced judgement and firm decisions made without fear or favour; for here, more than in any other area, powerful claims for the economic exploitation of the land will come into conflict with the primary purpose of the national park – to provide open-air enjoyment in a setting of unspoilt beauty for surrounding urban populations of exceptional density.'

The plaudits and awards mentioned above are a measure of the success with which the Peak National Park has pursued those objectives, and the words of Patrick Monkhouse, written in 1932, still ring true today: 'There has never been a time when more people were conscious of the beauty of (the Peak's) hills and dales, or when more people thought it a matter of public importance that beauty should remain beautiful.'

Thorpe Cloud, Dovedale. Proposed as a separate national park in the 1930s, Dovedale became part of the Peak National Park when it was designated in 1951.

Selected places of interest

The numbers after each place name are the map grid references to help readers locate the places mentioned. Ordnance Survey maps include instructions in the use of these grid references.

ARBOR LOW (SK 160635) Neolithic stone circle and henge, near Parsley Hay. Associated barrow at Gib Hill.

ASHFORD-IN-THE-WATER (SK 195697)
Limestone village, famous for well-dressings and medieval Sheepwash Bridge. Heavily restored church, with Norman doorway.

BAKEWELL (SK 218685) 'Capital' of the national park, and largest settlement (pop. 4,000). Popular Monday market, and agricultural show in early August. Information Centre, open all year, in Old Market Hall. Old House Folk Museum in Cunningham Place, and fourteenth century bridge over River Wye.

BRADWELL (SK 173812) Bustling limestone village under Bradwell Edge, famous for its home-made ice-cream and Bagshawe show cavern. Formerly important for lead mining, and the home of the 'Bradder beaver' hats, worn by generations of lead miners.

CASTLETON (SK 149825) Major tourist 'honeypot' of the Peak, with four show caverns, Peveril Castle, and shops selling rare Blue John jewellery. Information Centre, in Castle Street, open April-October and at winter weekends. Losehill Hall, the Park's residential study centre, is just outside the village.

CHATSWORTH (SK 261702) 'The Palace of the Peak', home of the Duke of Devonshire, in gracious parklands and gardens laid out by Sir Joseph Paxton. Attractions include a Children's Farmyard and Garden Centre.

EDALE (SK 133857) Walking centre of the Peak in shadow of Kinder Scout. Starting point of Pennine Way, with Information Centre open daily all year.

EYAM (SK 218764) Solid, lead-mining village under Eyam Edge, famous for the 'visitation' of the Great Plague in 1665/66 and with some fine examples of vernacular architecture, notably Eyam Hall, dated 1676. Many memorials to the tragedy in the village and church, and a splendid Saxon cross in the churchyard. Private museum in Lydgate.

HADDON HALL (SK 235663) One of England's finest medieval mansions, overlooking the Wye just outside Bakewell. Home of the Duke of Rutland, with memories of Dorothy Vernon's elopement and an oak-panelled banqueting hall and medieval chapel.

HARTINGTON (SK 128604) Dignified limestone village with large market square and 'mere'. Hartington Hall (1611), said to be visited by Bonnie Prince Charlie, is now a youth hostel. Stilton cheese factory just off main square.

HATHERSAGE (SK 230815) Fabled home of Little John, whose grave is alleged to be in the churchyard. Hathersage is convenient for visits to Carl Wark hillfort and North Lees Hall, the Thornfield Hall of *Jane Eyre*.

HOPE (SK 172835) Sprawling village after which the valley was named. Echoes of former medieval importance in its fine church, which has a Saxon cross in its churchyard. Agricultural market held every week.

LONGNOR (SK 088648) Another former market town, on the ridge between the Dove and Manifold, with cobbled market square and imposing Market Hall.

LYME HALL (SJ 964823) Palladian-style mansion – like a more grimy Chatsworth – on the edge of Stockport. Home of the Legh family, now in the hands of the National Trust. Fine moorland park setting with herd of red deer.

MONYASH (SK 150665) Typical nucleated limestone village, formerly important for lead mining, now for farming.

NINE LADIES STONE CIRCLE (SK 249635)
Bronze Age circle with associated King Stone, in a birch wood on Stanton Moor, near Birchover.

TIDESWELL (SK 152758) Splendid fourteenth century parish church is the highlight of this grey, important-looking village, high on the limestone plateau.

TISSINGTON (SK 175525) Pretty estate village with Jacobean hall (private) built for the FitzHerbert family. First well-dressings of the season (Ascension Day), and one of the earliest recorded accounts of this attractive custom.

WINSTER (SK 242605) Stone-arched Market House is now a National Trust information centre, and there are some fine Georgian houses.

YOULGREAVE (SK 212644) Church has one of the best towers (15th century) in the Peak, and the village, on the ridge between the Lathkill and the Bradford, has an urban air. Superb well-dressings in summer. Locally known as 'Pommy'.

Glossary

Barmote Court – lead miners' court, usually held twice a year

bellanded – poisoned by lead

Blue John – banded blue and white fluorspar

bole – early type of lead-smelting hearth

booth – herdsman's shelter or cow-shed

bovate – land measure, one-eighth of a carucate

Brigantes – Iron Age tribe of northern Britain

burh – fortified place

carucate – unit of land measurement in Danelaw

Celtic Fields – ancient field systems

clip – sheep shearing

clough – stream valley in Dark Peak

coe – shed of a lead miner, often covering a shaft

dale – a valley (Old Norse)

Derbyshire screws – local name for crinoid (sea lily) fossils

edge – steep cliff of Millstone Grit

gangue – waste minerals found with lead ore

Garlanding – ancient custom held in Castleton on Oak Apple Day (29th May)

grange – monastic farmstead

grough – natural drainage channel in peat

hag – bank of peat carved by groughs

hulm – island or water meadow (Danish)

Jagger – leader of a packhorse train

leadwort – spring sandwort, found on lead spoil heaps

ley – clearing in the forest (Old English)

low – a burial mound (Old English)

moss – a peat moor

nicking – taking over a lead mine not being worked

Pecsaetan – Anglo-Saxon tribe inhabiting Peak, 'hill dwellers'

pig – an ingot of lead

rake – a large vein of lead, often running for miles

scrin – a thin vein of lead, often branching from a rake

sough – drainage tunnel from a lead mine

squeezer – a stile in a drystone wall, formed by vertical slabs of stone

stowe – wooden windlass over a mine shaft

toadstone – volcanic rock or basalt

tor – rocky outcrop or hill (Old English)

t'owd man – ancient lead miners, or their workings

wapentake – a district, the Danelaw equivalent of a 'hundred', also used in lead mining areas

well – a spring or stream (Old English)

well-dressing – summer custom of decorating wells or springs with floral icons in thanks for water

Bibliography

Anderson, P and Shimwell D *Wild Flowers and other Plants of the Peak District*, Moorland, Ashbourne, 1981

Bramwell, D *Archaeology in the Peak District*, Moorland, Ashbourne, 1973

Bateman, Thomas *Ten Years' Diggings in Celtic and Saxon Grave-hills* (1861), Moorland, Ashbourne, 1978

Dodd, A E and E M *Peakland Roads and Trackways*, Moorland, Ashbourne, 1980

Edwards, K C *The Peak District*, Collins New Naturalist, London, 1962

Ekwall, Eilert *The Concise Oxford Dictionary of English Place-Names*, Oxford University Press, 1985

Ford, Trevor D *The Story of Peak District Rocks and Scenery*, East Midlands Region, the National Trust, Worksop, nd

Ford, Trevor D and Rieuwert, J H (ed) *Lead Mining in the Peak District*, Peak Park Joint Planning Board, Bakewell, 1983

Frost, R A *Birds of Derbyshire*, Moorland, Ashbourne, 1978

Harris, Helen *Industrial Archaeology of the Peak District*, David and Charles, Newton Abbot, 1971

Hart, C R *The North Derbyshire Archaeological Survey to AD 1500*, NDAT, Chesterfield, 1981

Millward, Roy and Robinson, Adrian *The Peak District*, Eyre Methuen, London, 1975

Morgan, Philip (ed) *Domesday Book, Derbyshire*, Phillimore, Chichester, 1978

Peak Park Joint Planning Board *National Park Plan*, PPJB, Bakewell, 1978

Smith, Roland *First and Last, the Peak National Park in words and pictures.* Peak Park Joint Planning Board, Bakewell, 1978

Wager, Jonathan F *Conservation of Historic Landscapes in the Peak District National Park*, Peak Park Joint Planning Board, Bakewell, 1981

Wolverson Cope, F *Geology Explained in the Peak District*, David and Charles, Newton Abbott, 1976

In addition, the Ordnance Survey's maps are essential to a proper, and safe, exploration of the area. The one-inch-to-the-mile Peak District Tourist map covers the whole of the Park in one sheet, while the two Outdoor Leisure maps at two-and-a-half inches to the mile, the Dark Peak and the White Peak, given even greater detail, down to field boundaries.